Little Knell

By the same author

The Religious Body
A Most Contagious Game
Henrietta Who?
The Complete Steel
A Late Phoenix
His Burial Too
Slight Mourning
Parting Breath
Some Die Eloquent
Passing Strange
Last Respects
Harm's Way
A Dead Liberty
The Body Politic
A Going Concern
Injury Time (Short Stories)
After Effects
Stiff News

Little Knell

Catherine Aird

ST. MARTIN'S MINOTAUR ❦ NEW YORK

www.minotaurbooks.com

ISBN 0-312-26983-8

First published in Great Britain by Macmillan, an imprint of Macmillan Publishers Ltd

First U.S. Edition: April 2001

10 9 8 7 6 5 4 3 2 1

For Emily Abbey with love

Chapter One

Spine Broken

'Wake up there, boy, or you'll have us both over.' Sidney Wetherspoon grasped the lid of an ottoman as it suddenly canted over in the direction of his youthful assistant.

'Sorry,' said Wayne Goddard sullenly.

'Easy, now, round the corner,' exhorted Sid, who had begun to puff slightly. 'Take it gently on the bend.'

Wayne Goddard obediently changed his working pace from slow to dead slow.

'It wouldn't do for us to break anything. Not here.' The older man took advantage of the pause while he spoke. 'Even though, me, I'd ten times rather clear a house when someone's died than when they haven't.'

'I don't like being stood over neither.' The youth sniffed, responding to the thought rather than the statement. 'Can't stand it, myself. Gives me the willies.'

'It still wouldn't do for us to be breaking anything here.' Wetherspoon peered round the room. 'Not in Whimbrel House.'

'Too right it wouldn't.' Wayne Goddard yawned. He had been sent by the Job Centre on a month's trial to Wetherspoon and Wetherspoon, Furniture Removers

1

Ltd. of Railway Street, Berebury, and deemed it prudent to be polite to his employers. To begin with, anyway.

'All this stuff here might look like a load of old rope to you, lad . . .' said Sid Wetherspoon expansively, waving a horny hand round the spacious room which they were now clearing.

'Smells like it anyway,' muttered Goddard under his breath. 'Could do with a proper airing, if you ask me.'

' . . . but there's them, I can tell you, that think it's valuable enough.'

'You could have fooled me.' Goddard shrugged his shoulders, his expression managing to convey at one and the same time both total disinterest and considerable scepticism. He certainly wasn't going to admit that he was actually standing in the oddest room he had ever been in during his short life. It was full – completely full – of fusty trophies of travels to out-of-the way places, travels that had clearly taken place a long, long time ago.

'Very valuable,' insisted Sid, correctly reading the young man's mind. 'I'm telling you.'

'What, even that stuffed alligator?' Wayne raised an eyebrow. He had been practising raising one eyebrow as a gesture of disbelief ever since he had seen it done by the manager of the Job Centre who had been listening to Wayne's latest – and completely specious – tale of woe.

'Even that stuffed alligator.' Having now succeeded in getting his breath back, the older man bent forward and applied himself again to lifting the intricately carved sandalwood ottoman whose great weight had brought about his respiratory distress in the first place.

'Get away!' said Wayne.

'I dare say,' said Wetherspoon drily. 'Now, you just roll your sleeves up and take the other end of this here prize piece and go first and then pitch over there.'

Wayne Goddard applied himself to the sweet-smelling wooden chest but without enthusiasm – and without rolling up his sleeves either.

'Hey,' shouted Sid Wetherspoon, having successfully negotiated the ottoman round a suit of armour. 'Use both your hands and watch what you're doing with your end.'

'I am,' said Goddard untruthfully. Since he was the one of the pair walking backwards, he could perforce do no such thing as look where he was going. While once he wouldn't have hesitated to have said so – with various rich and quite unprintable embellishments – today he held his peace. There had been a glint in the eye under that raised eyebrow at the Job Centre which he hadn't liked. It had betokened a very real willingness to take matters further and cut off his benefits if Goddard, W. G., didn't hold this latest job down.

'I reckon,' said Wetherspoon, jerking his shoulder in the direction of a long woven silk rug elegantly stretched out against the further wall, 'that that's worth a pretty penny, too, to someone who really wants it.'

'You're joking.' Goddard shrugged.

'To say nothing of that stuffed object in the glass case in the corner,' carried on Sid. 'Whatever it might be when it's at home.'

'Looks like a dead duck to me,' opined Wayne, who had never seen a hoopoe – dead or alive – before.

'Else,' reasoned Sid Wetherspoon realistically, 'why do you think they've got their solicitor and their chief legatee over here while we do a simple removal job?'

'Search me,' said Wayne Goddard indifferently.

'I wouldn't put that past them either,' said Sid sardonically. 'Not this pair, anyway.'

'You mean Mr Puckle?' asked Wayne.

'How come you know Mr Puckle?' asked Sid curiously. He made a mental note to check on the lad's references when he got back to the office. They couldn't be doing with a maverick in the company.

'I've been around, haven't I?' uttered Wayne, a truculent look coming over his face.

'So it would seem,' said Sid, conducting a rapid reappraisal of the suitability of Wetherspoon and Wetherspoon's new recruit for a permanent position in the old firm.

'That one's called Simon,' Wayne informed him. 'He's from that lot with offices down by the bridge. You know, Puckle, Puckle and Nunnery.' He sniffed. 'Not that you'd know it from their brass plate. You can't read it any more. Worn out by polishing.'

'Old established.' Sid nodded. The firm of Wetherspoon and Wetherspoon had begun with a horse and cart in Sid's grandfather's day which made the removal men johnnys-come-lately in comparison with the law practice. 'Always been around here in Berebury, the Puckles.'

'And always making money out of other people's

misfortunes,' added Wayne Goddard bitterly, wiping a watery eye.

'Well . . .' Sid took the opportunity to lower the ottoman to the floor once more while he considered this.

Wayne wrinkled up his nose. 'That's all that solicitors do, isn't it? Prey on the unlucky.'

'They'll be making money all right here at Whimbrel House,' said Sid Wetherspoon, deciding not to enquire too closely into how Wayne Goddard had come to know so much about the members of the local legal profession at his tender age.

'I'll bet.' Goddard seconded this warmly.

'They do say,' went on Sid profoundly, 'that some rain falls in every life though I couldn't tell you about the misfortune bit, I'm sure.' He screwed up his face in an effort of recollection. 'I must say I've never heard of old Colonel Caversham having had more than his fair share of trouble in this world.'

'Lucky sod him, then,' said Goddard, making it quite clear that he thought he'd already had his own mede of difficulties.

'The only trouble the colonel had,' said Sid doggedly, 'was in dying. From all accounts he took his time about that.'

Goddard pointed across the room. 'Bet those two vultures over there didn't lose interest. Not nohow.'

'No,' agreed Sid fairly. 'They stuck around all right, and when the old boy did die at last they gave us all this work.'

'But,' admitted Goddard, who was not interested in

anyone who was old let alone dead, still gazing across the big room, 'I don't know who the guy with Mr Puckle is. The geezer in the dark blue jacket and brown moccasins . . .'

'That,' said Sid Wetherspoon impressively, 'is our Mr Marcus Fixby-Smith.'

'And who's he when he comes out from under all that hair?'

Wetherspoon looked across at the man with the middling flowing locks and then back at Wayne's skinhead haircut and decided he didn't greatly care for either style. 'Mr Fixby-Smith over there is the Curator of the Greatorex Museum in Granary Row.'

'Can't afford a good barber, I suppose.' Wayne's glance travelled appraisingly over the other man, taking in with a certain contempt the expensive grey woollen polo-neck jumper and well-cut blue denim jeans the curator was wearing.

'I expect he likes that floppy fringe,' said Sid slyly. 'Keeps his head warm.'

'He's out of touch, that's all,' said Wayne Goddard loftily. He himself was wearing a dark green Puffa jacket over a long-sleeved grubby white T-shirt.

'Is he now? Well, I never . . .' Sid had already noticed that Wayne's T-shirt was sporting a motif which had struck him as vaguely obscene. It was accompanied by blue shell-suit trousers and a pair of old trainers which might once have been white. If so, it was a long time ago.

'Doesn't he know,' remarked Wayne largely, 'that all that gear is right out now?'

'Don't suppose so,' said his new employer equably. 'Museums aren't what you might call up to date.'

'Marked down everywhere, those clothes.'

Neither Sidney Wetherspoon nor Marcus Fixby-Smith would have ever credited the total retail price of Wayne's current outfit. The manager of the Job Centre, though, knew what it would have cost down to the last penny – in the unlikely event, that is, of its having been bought over the counter for real money.

'You don't say,' murmured Sid, who didn't ever buy new clothes until his wife made him.

'So what's that man doing here with Mr Puckle, then?' asked Wayne Goddard. He had cottoned on very quickly to the fact that his new employer preferred standing and talking to lifting heavy furniture.

So did Wayne.

'Making sure that he gets his pound of flesh from the colonel's leavings, I expect,' said Wetherspoon, 'seeing as how the museum's been left all the non-literary artefacts in the colonel's unsecured estate.'

'What's unsecured estate?' asked Wayne alertly.

'Not what you think, my boy,' retorted Sid. 'It means what the colonel could leave as he wanted to. Not tied up for his heirs and successors.'

'Who gets the rest then?'

'You may well ask,' said Sid enigmatically. 'The other thing that pair over there are doing,' he added without heat, 'is making quite sure that we don't get any of this unsecured stuff either.'

'Wouldn't have thought you'd have wanted any of it anyway,' said Wayne Goddard, unwittingly at one and the same time sealing his own long-term future in the removal trade and making more work for the manager of the Berebury Job Centre. 'Looks like a real load of old tat to me.'

'It's all souvenirs of primitive places,' said Sid, casting an appraising glance at the various spots on Wayne's anatomy where his skin had been pierced for the suspension of gold ornaments, 'where the natives stuck rings into their noses and ears. They didn't know any better, of course,' he added with a straight face. 'Not being civilized like us.'

The irony passed Goddard by. 'You'd never get anyone to buy any of this rubbish off you if you did half-inch it . . .'

'I should imagine that Mr Fixby-Smith is here, like Mr Puckle, in his professional capacity,' said Sid, deciding against trying to explain to Wayne that it wasn't the custom of Wetherspoon and Wetherspoon to help themselves to the goods they were removing – good or bad.

'Big deal,' said Wayne Goddard laconically.

'In which capacity,' said Sid Wetherspoon, bending once more to the sandalwood ottoman, 'he has inherited this pretty little lot here. It's all going to the museum seeing as how it's of anthropological interest.'

'All of it?'

'So Mr Puckle says. And he should know because he's paying us. Puckle, Puckle and Nunnery are the colonel's executors.'

'Even that spear on the wall?'

'Assegai,' said the removal man knowledgeably.

'Used to see quite a lot of them about in the old days. Colonials coming home.'

'Offensive weapon within the meaning of the Act is what the magistrates would call that,' said Wayne Goddard, equably knowledgeable, but in a rather different field. 'A bladed instrument.'

'I don't care what they would call it,' said Wetherspoon flatly. 'If Puckle, Puckle and Nunnery are paying us to take it over to the museum, then that's where it goes – all of it. And nowhere else. Understood?'

'Understood.'

'Including that rather valuable brass tray over there that has come to Calleshire from Birmingham by way of Benares.'

'But who gets the money?' persisted Wayne.

'That I don't rightly know.' Sid's lips came together in a tight clamp. 'That's family business. Now, get going or we'll never get shot of this job.'

'But, Sid . . .'

'Mr Wetherspoon to you,' said Sid sternly. 'Unless, that is,' he added from long experience in the removals business, 'you were ever to drop anything on my foot and then you could call me whatever you like because you wouldn't be around long enough for me to hear you. Understood?'

'Yes, Si—Mr Wetherspoon.'

'And mind that Ali Baba vase as you go. We should have moved it out of the way before we started on this chest. They can come valuable, too.' He looked disparagingly down at the youth. 'I dare say you know all about Ali Baba and the Forty Thieves, don't you?'

Wayne Goddard grinned for the first time that day. 'Yes, Mr Wetherspoon.'

'I thought you might. Now, take your end gently round the doorway and then we'll have another rest. It's heavy enough.'

'Yes, Mr Wetherspoon.'

They were interrupted by a pleasant voice from the other end of the room. 'I say, Sid, can you spare a minute?'

'Coming, Mr Puckle.' Sid immediately lowered the ottoman again, this time answering to his Christian name without hesitation. Puckle, Puckle and Nunnery put a lot of good business in the way of Wetherspoon and Wetherspoon; far too much for Sid to be standing on ceremony with the solicitor.

'Mr Fixby-Smith here tells me that there's something at Whimbrel House that needs rather specialized lifting.' Simon Puckle was standing beside the museum curator. They were both staring down at something on the floor, and if the solicitor recognized Wayne Goddard, he gave no sign of it. 'It's just here.'

Sid dusted off his hands and walked over to the two men with a certain amount of curiosity. He'd seen nothing in his preliminary look round the house that had struck him as a particular problem. 'What's that, then? Something extra?'

'Rodoheptah,' said Marcus Fixby-Smith.

'Come again?' said Sid.

'This sarcophagus here,' explained the museum curator, indicating a long wooden oblong object at his feet.

'Ah, so that's what that is, is it?' said Sid easily. 'I hadn't reckoned on that being too difficult to lift myself. It doesn't look it.'

'Not difficult,' amplified Marcus Fixby-Smith. 'Important. Mr Howard Air – he's my committee chairman – is very pleased we've come into all this . . .'

'Ah.' Sid let out a long breath. 'That explains it.' In their time Wetherspoon and Wetherspoon had effortlessly moved countless objects deemed by their owners to be important as well as difficult to lift. He regarded the painted wooden object with professional interest. The colours had faded to the palest of pinks and greys. 'Valuable, is it?'

'Very,' said Fixby-Smith shortly. 'To us, anyway. It's an Egyptian mummy and it should put the Greatorex Museum on the map at long last.'

'You mean,' said Wayne Goddard, finding something in his day's work of interest at long last, 'that there's a body in there?'

'Probably,' said the museum curator, quite unconcerned, 'but we won't be able to be absolutely sure the grave robbers haven't been into it first until it's been X-rayed and we've seen the bones.'

Simon Puckle said by way of explanation, 'Colonel Caversham brought it back from one of his first journeys of exploration in the Middle East . . .'

'Exact provenance unknown, though,' put in Marcus Fixby-Smith, quoting from a long list in his hand.

' . . . where,' continued the solicitor, 'it was not

11

unknown for English travellers to be sold empty sar-
cophagi.'

'I'll bet,' said Wayne Goddard in spite of himself.

Simon Puckle gave a deprecating cough. 'It must
also be said that it was equally the case in those days
that on occasion . . .' He paused and amended this. ' . . .
quite often, returning English travellers chose to declare
the sarcophagus they were shipping home to be – er –
unoccupied to facilitate their getting it through customs.'

'Can't trust anyone, can you?' marvelled Wayne
Goddard.

'I see on the executors' schedule here,' the museum
curator waved his list in the air in the direction of Simon
Puckle, 'that it has been described as "one sarcophagus,
exact contents unknown". '

'Precisely,' responded the solicitor. 'We, although we
are acting for the Colonel's estate, don't really know
what's in there. That is, we are not in a position to say
with any degree of certainty.'

'However,' announced Marcus Fixby-Smith firmly,
'for the purposes of removing this artefact from here to
the Greatorex Museum I am deeming it to contain the
remains of a human being rightly or wrongly given
the name of Rodoheptah, since this is what the colonel
called it.'

'Quite so,' murmured Simon Puckle.

'What does that mean exactly?' asked Sid, wiping his
hands on his trousers, the better to take hold of the
wooden case.

'That we carry it very carefully,' said Fixby-Smith.

He was a man to whom the use of the Royal we came easily.

'Like we knew there was someone in there?' asked Wayne. He looked distinctly dubious.

'Just like that,' said Fixby-Smith. 'A someone moreover who might come to harm if he were tipped up.'

'Or even tilted,' growled Sid Wetherspoon, who had a good idea of what the firm's insurers would have to say about any claim arising for damages to the skeleton of a long-dead Egyptian.

'How do you know it's a he?' asked Wayne. He had already sensed that his employment with the removal firm wasn't going to last any longer than it had done with all the other jobs he had tried. 'Could have been a woman, couldn't it?'

'Not with that name ending,' replied Fixby-Smith absently.

'Use your eyes, lad.' Sid pointed to a phallic design still just discernible on the mummy case.

'What? Oh, I see . . .' At the drop of a hat Wayne's face assumed a look of unbelievable innocence. 'Blue for a boy . . .'

'That's enough of that, Goddard,' snapped Sid Wetherspoon. 'Here, take your end and get moving.'

Wayne Goddard grinned cheekily as he bent down. 'What you might call dead weight, eh?'

Wetherspoon, ignoring this, turned to Simon Puckle and Marcus Fixby-Smith and said with dignity, 'I can assure you, gentlemen, that moving the mummy will be no problem at all.'

Moving the mummy was a problem somewhere else, though.

The police station at Berebury.

But later.

Chapter Two

Bumped

'Detective Inspector Sloan?' enquired the man's voice at the other end of the telephone. 'Jenkins here. Customs and Excise, Kinnisport.'

'Good morning,' said Sloan warily. The police force were not the only regulatory body in the kingdom deeply concerned with the pursuit of wrongdoers. Customs and Excise ranked high among the others.

And knew it.

'Just a courtesy call . . .'

'Ah . . .' Detective Inspector C. D. Sloan was head of the tiny Criminal Investigation Department of F Division of the Calleshire Constabulary, and such troubles as there were in the market town of Berebury and its rural environs usually landed on his desk; but not those offshore. They were the province of the water guard.

The exciseman gave a little laugh. 'From one brother-in-law to another, you might say.'

'Quite,' responded Sloan, acknowledging the witticism. The poet Robert Burns had been an exciseman; perhaps Jenkins too saw himself as having a way with words.

'Or to fellow labourers in the vineyard.'

Actually, this was generous of Jenkins since Customs and Excise enjoyed powers of search – let alone other things – envied by both the police and the Inland Revenue.

'About a man called Boller at Edsway. Horace Boller,' said Jenkins. 'Do you people know him?'

'The boatman? Oh, yes, we know Boller all right.' The Boller family had been twisting the people of Edsway since time immemorial. 'An old rogue if ever there was one; always in a very small way, though. Never does anything you can actually pin on him.'

'That's the man,' said Jenkins at once.

'What's he done now?' If the excise people had caught out Horace Boller in malfeasance then they were better men than the entire Calleshire Constabulary who had signally failed to catch out Boller performing any action that constituted a chargeable offence. And not for want of trying, either.

'We're not sure that he's done anything,' said the man from Customs and Excise frankly. 'Well, that is to say nothing that we can nail him for.'

'So?'

'I don't know what it was like with you inland, Inspector, but it was pretty foggy out at sea this morning . . .'

'A little misty here, that's all,' said Sloan, waiting.

'Boller was attending to his lobster pots off the headland early today when he fished something up in one of them.'

'Something interesting swam into it while he wasn't looking, then?' Sloan tried to hurry the man along.

Customs and Excise were very much the longest-established service, and now and then inclined to rub it in.

'Something valuable, Inspector,' said Jenkins. 'Something very valuable indeed. And not a lobster.'

'Drugs?' said Sloan, beginning to get irritated with the other man's circumlocution.

'Four kilos of just that,' said Jenkins with satisfaction. 'It's gone for analysis, of course, but we're sure enough it's heroin.'

'I see,' said Sloan. He wasn't surprised by the information. They'd worked out long ago that the drugs that percolated out all over the county of Calleshire were coming in by sea. 'And Boller handed it in just like that?' Now that was something that did surprise him.

'Boller told us that he didn't know what it was or how it came to be in one of his lobster pots.'

'And did he know?'

'Ah, Inspector, that's a horse of a very different colour. You see, there just happened to be one of our own vessels about at the time, and it hove in view out of the fog just as Boller was hauling his catch in. He hadn't known we were lying off the headland and, because of the poor visibility, we hadn't realized how near he was to us.'

'And so Boller turned Queen's Evidence pretty quickly, just to be on the safe side?' He'd never known any man so good at minding his own back as Horace Boller.

Jenkins laughed again. 'I reckon he didn't have much choice about doing his Little Jack Horner act because he saw us see him at it.'

' "What a good boy am I",' quoted Sloan absently, thinking hard.

'He pulled out a plum, all right,' said Jenkins. 'The street value of this little lot doesn't bear thinking about; although how the dealers use the money they make from the stuff without it showing beats me.'

'Us, too. All the businesses we know here are doing well but not so well as we'd want to know the reason why.'

'Somebody's getting the money,' said the Customs and Excise man ineluctably.

'Undoubtedly, but you tell me who and we'll run them in. No problem.'

'And getting rid of the takings pretty quickly too – well before we catch 'em with it, anyway.'

'And, as far as we know,' persisted Sloan, undeflected, 'all the local solicitors and accountants are as upright as pianos.'

'And the insurance people?'

'How can anyone tell?'

'It must be big money. Really big.'

'I don't doubt it,' the policeman said.

Detective Inspector Sloan had decided years ago that all policemen had to live strictly compartmentalized lives. At his own breakfast table only this morning there had been a lengthy debate – well, discussion, anyway – on whether or not the Sloan household's budget would run to the purchase of a special collection of patio standard roses. His wife, Margaret, had been markedly unsympathetic.

It wasn't so much a matter of guns before butter,

she had remarked, as butter before roses. Hanging heavily over the talk had been the unresolved matter of a new floor covering to replace the worn one in the Sloan kitchen.

And now here he was at work, having taken a quantum leap in relative values, talking not only about drugs worth a king's ransom on the open market but the manifold difficulties of stashing the proceeds away. He said more to himself than to the customs man, 'It's a funny old world, all right.'

'And Boller was innocence personified when we interviewed him. Couldn't have been more virtuous.'

'Naturally,' murmured Sloan. 'It's not as if he could very well be anything else if he was caught in the act.'

'Does a good job, does our revenue cutter,' said Jenkins with satisfaction. 'Smugglers don't like it at all.'

'And Boller?'

'Don't worry, Inspector. We kept a bit of an eye on him afterwards. He parked the lobsters he had caught . . .'

'The real ones?'

'The decapod crustaceans themselves,' Jenkins assured him solemnly. 'He put them in a tank of water and then he took a basket of bits of fish over to that animal rescue place behind Edsway. You know where I mean – the one those two women run.'

'Alison and Jennifer Kirk.' What with their fund-raising and their good works all Calleshire knew about the animal sanctuary at Edsway. The two sisters took in the stray dogs and cats that were brought into the police station, too.

'The spare fish is for the cats there. One of my men says Boller always does that whenever he's got anything unsaleable in his catch.'

'And there was I,' said Detective Inspector Sloan sourly, 'thinking that Horace Boller was the exception that proves the rule about there being some good in every man.'

But the Customs and Excise officer was following quite a different train of thought.

'Our picking up this consignment will make a big hole in some dealer's distribution system,' he forecast. 'I don't know how many weeks' supply it constituted for your patch, Inspector Sloan, but I dare say you're going to feel the shortage over at Berebury quite soon. That can be quite tricky.'

'Yes,' said Sloan, bleakly.

'Anyway,' Jenkins finished breezily before he rang off, 'now we've let you know all about it.'

The civilities had been duly observed.

It wasn't the diplomatic niceties of inter-regulatory authority communication which were troubling Super-intendent Leeyes. It was a matter of protocol. He barely listened to Sloan's report about Horace Boller before unburdening himself about another, more press-ing, problem.

'It's the coroner,' Leeyes rasped.

'The coroner, sir?' said Sloan.

'Making work.'

'Really, sir?' Sloan didn't know what to think about

this. The trouble was that the superintendent – an absolutist if ever there was one – only ever saw difficulties from his own point of view, which made even a well-educated guess impossible.

'The man can't have enough to do,' grumbled Leeyes. 'That's his trouble.'

Detective Inspector Sloan contented himself with leaning forward attentively. There was absolutely nothing in his expression to indicate that he was taking this last assertion with the proverbial pinch of salt. He did not himself suppose for one moment that Her Majesty's Coroner for East Calleshire, Mr Granville Locombe-Stableford, had nothing better to do than upset the police superintendent, whatever that worthy might think. He did know, though, that the coroner and Superintendent Leeyes were sparring partners of old. And he knew, too, that in the way of ancient enemies, the two of them picked a quarrel whenever they could find a bone even half worth the contention.

All Sloan said aloud though was, 'I'm not aware, sir, of there having been any reportable deaths in the division today . . .'

'There haven't,' snapped Leeyes.

'But . . .'

'Don't you understand, Sloan? That's just what I'm telling you. The man hasn't got better things to do and all this does is prove it.'

'This?' Sloan picked on the word, feeling as if he was grasping at a straw in the verbal – and proverbial – wind. 'What . . .'

But Leeyes had already taken off at a tangent.

'Poking his nose into matters that have nothing whatsoever to do with him; that's what he's doing.'

'You mean, sir,' advanced Sloan cautiously, trying again, 'that there's been a fatality in East Calleshire but that it's outside Mr Locombe-Stableford's jurisdiction?' This at least, decided Sloan, would make sense. A deep preoccupation with the territorial imperative was one of the many characteristics which the superintendent and the coroner had in common.

'Well, no,' hedged Leeyes. 'Not exactly.'

'Or outside ours?' suggested Sloan even more cautiously. The superintendent knew to an inch where his own writ ran and defended all his boundaries with a vigour that some of his staff thought might well have been better devoted to more important police matters.

'No,' admitted Leeyes grudgingly. 'This body's on our patch all right. No doubt about that.'

'And on the coroner's, too?' asked Sloan, puzzled. He ran his mind's eye down the list that reposed on his desk, new every morning, of missing persons in Calleshire. As he remembered it, the names comprised those of a confused elderly gentleman who had gone absent from an old people's home in Kinnisport – and without his false teeth, too, which his carers considered significant; a young woman who hadn't been seen since a tiff with her boyfriend – the boyfriend had been interviewed and would be interviewed again if she didn't turn up soon; and a now-not-so-young woman who hadn't been observed by the constabulary on her usual beat on the streets of Luston for the last six nights.

'That's the trouble,' said Leeyes.

'I don't quite follow, sir.'

'The coroner says,' the superintendent mimicked the carefully modulated tones of that august official, 'that acting on information received . . .'

'What!' Sloan exclaimed. 'Sorry, sir, but . . .'

'I thought you wouldn't like that, Sloan,' observed the superintendent with a certain melancholy satisfaction.

He didn't. That phrase, 'acting on information received', was one of the police's best lines; not usually one of the coroner's.

'Mr Locombe-Stableford says,' went on the superintendent, 'he's been informed that a body has been moved within his jurisdiction in East Calleshire, but without his knowledge or consent.'

'And the name of the deceased?' asked Detective Inspector Sloan, getting out his notebook. As far as he was concerned, any of the three souls on this morning's list of local missing could have turned up anywhere in Calleshire as dead bodies rather than as living persons.

Or none of them.

'Nobody knows the name for certain,' said the superintendent enigmatically.

'An unidentified body . . .' began Sloan.

'But I am told,' continued Leeyes, 'that ever since anyone can remember he has been known as Rodoheptah.'

'Would you happen to know how that was spelt, sir?' Sloan metaphorically licked the tip of his pencil and waited.

'No,' said Leeyes.

'Is it known, then, where the deceased was removed from, sir?'

Leeyes squinted down at a piece of paper on his desk. 'Whimbrel House, Edgewood Hill, Staple St James.'

'Colonel Caversham's?' Sloan looked up, surprised. 'But it's weeks and weeks since he died. Quite a famous old boy in his time . . .'

'Not as long ago as this body,' said Leeyes grimly. 'It's an Egyptian mummy.'

'But . . .'

'But our Mr Granville Locombe-Stableford insists that as far as he is concerned a mummy is nevertheless still a body.'

'Within the meaning of the Act, I suppose,' supplemented Detective Inspector Sloan, not sure exactly where this got them. He, himself, was still trying to concentrate all his working hours on the sudden and worrying upsurge in drug dealing in rural Calleshire. Knowing that the stuff was coming in by sea hadn't really got them much further.

'Precisely,' agreed Leeyes eagerly. 'That is until the remains have been duly certified by a registered medical practitioner as being only of archaeological interest.' Leeyes completed the coroner's grounds for jurisdiction in a manner that left no room for doubt about his opinion of them.

With an effort, Sloan wrenched his mind off the drug scene. 'So . . .'

'So, Sloan, as far as the coroner is concerned, technically, an offence was committed when the body was moved from where it last was.'

'I see.' Sloan cast about in the back of his mind for the exact nature of this offence. If anyone was going to be charged with it, he, Sloan, would first have to find out under which particular ancient statute that would be; and that would certainly have to be done before he even got as far as cautioning anyone. He had an uneasy feeling that the office of coroner went back to William the Conqueror, at least. 'Do we know who committed this alleged offence, sir?'

'Wetherspoon and Wetherspoon.'

'The removal people?'

'Them,' said Leeyes. 'Or, more precisely, Sidney Wetherspoon himself and one Wayne Goddard.'

'Wayne Goddard?' Sloan frowned. 'That name rings a bell. Sid Wetherspoon, I've known since I was a lad.' Detective Inspector Christopher Dennis Sloan was Calleshire born and bred and thus knew his patch better than most. 'I wouldn't have thought he'd do the wrong thing. Not Sid.'

The superintendent picked up the message sheet and continued, quoting from the coroner's statement, ' . . . "in that they did move or cause to be moved a body without either first obtaining my written permission or acting on the duly authorized instructions of my officer". '

'So,' concluded Detective Inspector Sloan, 'he's not blaming PC Stuart, then?' Police Constable Douglas Stuart had acted as the coroner's officer, his right-hand man, at Berebury for years and years.

'Not likely,' snorted Leeyes. 'Well, he wouldn't, would he, seeing he needs him like he does? Locombe-

Stableford hasn't done a hand's turn himself since Nelson lost his eye.'

'Doug Stuart does save him a lot of work,' observed Sloan moderately.

'Difficult man to pin anything on, is Stuart,' said Leeyes, sounding aggrieved. As far as the superintendent was concerned this was the rub.

'Where was this body going?' asked Sloan, since there was no point in getting embroiled in differing views of Douglas Stuart. As Sloan had confirmed for himself a long time ago, one man looked up and saw stars and another looked down and saw mud. Stars or mud, he would talk to Stuart first.

'Not going,' said Leeyes gloomily. 'Gone. And that's only half the trouble.'

Sloan raised an eyebrow interrogatively.

The trouble with the drug dealing that was so much on his mind was that it had suddenly burgeoned out over Calleshire from the urban area around the industrial town of Luston. And that was what he should be working on now. He hadn't time to be playing about with arcane old statutes for sake of an outworn argument.

'It's already been taken over to the Greatorex Museum,' said Leeyes. 'And Marcus Fixby-Smith – apparently he's the head honcho over there – won't play ball.'

Detective Inspector Sloan said he could see that there might be difficulties.

'Difficulties!' trumpeted Leeyes. 'You haven't started to appreciate quite how many difficulties there are yet, Sloan.'

'Sorry, sir.'

'Apparently, the curator doesn't want to part with the mummy because exactly how you first begin to go about examining these old things is very important.'

Sloan said that he could see that it might be.

'And he doesn't want anyone else messing about with it until he and his archaeological pals have had a go.'

Sloan said he could see that, too.

'You may be able to, Sloan,' said Leeyes with heat. 'All I can say is that the coroner can't.' He sniffed. 'Or won't.'

'Do we know what it is exactly Mr Locombe-Stableford wants?' asked Sloan. Something – he didn't know quite what yet – didn't add up here. Especially that business about acting on information received. That sort of information usually reached the police long before it got to the coroner.

'Trouble, that's what he wants,' muttered Leeyes, tersely. 'If you ask me, he's out for blood. Preferably mine. And, as he never fails to remind me, he has the last word.'

That was the other rub.

'So, Sloan,' carried on Leeyes, 'you'd better get over to the museum and sort things out as quickly as possible.' He paused and added with a fine show of magnanimity, 'You can take Constable Crosby with you. We don't need him here today.'

Chapter Three

Defective

'Hullo, there!' hollered Horace Boller, as he pushed open the dilapidated wicker gate at the Calleshire Animal Sanctuary at Edsway.

He was greeted by a cacophony of barks from the assorted dogs in residence.

'Quiet!' he bellowed.

This made the dogs bark even more loudly.

Usually, by this time, a woman's head would have come round the back door with the offer of a mug of tea and a shouted command to the dogs to surcease. Horace suspected that his usual welcome at the animal rescue place owed more to the fish he brought with him than to himself, but he did not very much care. A mug of tea was, after all, a mug of tea. And, anyway, stinking fish would have been a nuisance to him in his cottage, let alone to his neighbours.

He advanced on the back door, calling out, 'Anyone at home?' There was still no response but the door was ajar so he let himself in. Unexpectedly, he found the two sisters who ran the sanctuary sitting at the kitchen table doing nothing. This was so uncharacteristic of them in the middle of the day that he looked from one to the other and asked, 'What's up?'

Alison Kirk, the elder of the two, answered him. 'We've had a bit of bad news, Horace.'

Boller set his creel down in the kitchen sink and accepted the proffered mug of tea. 'Your nephew?' he said.

She nodded, brushing a solitary tear from her cheek. 'Derek, our sister's son.'

'He died yesterday,' said Jennifer Kirk, harder-hearted and dry-eyed.

'Poor boy,' said Alison. 'I'm glad now his mother isn't still alive.'

'Silly fool,' said Jennifer.

'You shouldn't say that, Jennifer.' Alison admonished her sister. 'We don't know what makes people be like Derek. It isn't as if he could have helped being like he was.'

'He knew the score,' said Jennifer Kirk.

'He knew there was no hope,' said Alison, while Horace spooned a large quantity of sugar into his tea. 'They told him up at the hospital months ago that they couldn't do any more for him.'

'Just to go on taking the tablets,' said Jennifer astringently.

'And that wasn't easy,' protested the older and gentler Alison. 'He had to take so many of them you see, Horace. Thirty a day, would you believe it?'

Horace nodded behind his mug of tea.

'But like it says in the Bible,' said Jennifer, 'as you sow, so shall you reap.'

29

'I really do think you should be a little more charitable, dear,' murmured her sister.

'He did sow some wild oats, though,' said Jennifer. 'And in some funny places.'

'And how!' muttered Horace under his breath.

Alison, who hadn't heard what he'd said, went on. 'Don't forget, Jennifer, that there, but for the grace of God, go us all.'

Jennifer gave a rather unladylike snort. 'I think it's really rather unlikely in the circumstances that either of us could ever have behaved like Derek.'

'And in any case,' said Alison, ducking this issue, 'one shouldn't speak ill of the dead.'

Horace Boller offered what comfort lay within his own hedonistic philosophy. 'He had a good run for his money anyway.'

'Yes, that was nice, wasn't it,' said Alison Kirk sentimentally. 'That he could enjoy his last year like he did, I mean. He even gave us some money for the sanctuary.'

'Well, as Derek so often said,' commented Jennifer drily, 'he couldn't take it with him.'

'He lived it up while he could,' grunted Horace Boller, refilling his mug without asking. 'Or so they told me over at the Ornum Arms at Almstone.'

'It was one of his favourite places,' said Alison wistfully. 'He really liked it there. It was very popular, he told us. Lots of people he knew always in the bar . . .'

Jennifer Kirk remained unimpressed. 'Drink never helped anyone. And not him, ever.'

'If you want all your cats to have a bit of fish,' interrupted Horace Boller, pointing in the direction of the basket he had brought, 'then you'd better get that big ginger tom off it pretty smartish.'

'We've got to go where, sir?' Detective Constable William Edward Crosby, by no means the brightest star in the detective firmament of F Division, was always keen to travel anywhere, provided only that he could drive a police car there at the fastest possible speed.

'The Greatorex Museum,' said Sloan, adding by way of self-preservation that there was no hurry about getting there. 'No hurry at all, Crosby, seeing that what we're going over to the museum to take a look at has been dead and gone a very long time and is still in its coffin.'

By rights, Detective Sergeant Gelven, competent and experienced, should have been at his right hand but Detective Sergeant Gelven had gone sick of the police palsy or its modern-day equivalent and Sloan had been left with Detective Constable Crosby, inexperienced and incompetent, in his stead.

'And what we should actually be doing,' said Sloan tightly, 'is anticipating the trouble likely to be caused by a sudden and severe shortage of heroin in our patch and doing something about it ahead of the action.'

'I don't see why that should be our worry, sir.' Crosby pulled the steering wheel round with two fingers of one hand before remembering that both hands should have been on the wheel in the classic ten minutes to two o'clock hold. He hastily assumed this position.

'Oh, you don't, don't you?' said Sloan with some acerbity. 'And why not, may I ask?'

'Because the junkies can't get their hands on the heroin if it's safely over at the analysts.'

'Had it occurred to you, Crosby, that if the new supplies aren't available, something might happen to the price of what stock the dealers have still got?'

The constable changed down a gear for a tight bend ahead. 'It'll go up, I suppose.'

'It will go up by leaps and bounds. And,' Sloan forecasted, 'something else will happen to it, too.'

'Sir?'

'It'll be adulterated down to make it seem to go further. And that, Crosby, means trouble. Big trouble. All round.'

'But, surely, sir,' Crosby objected naively, 'that's not our problem either.'

'Think again,' advised Sloan.

'It's not us who are buying the stuff.' He sounded mulish now. 'It's the addicts.'

'For starters,' spelled out Sloan, 'it means much more acquisitive crime in the area to raise money to pay the dealers more for a less pure drug . . .'

'Yes, sir, but . . .'

'Remember, the heroin habit is still going to need feeding whatever the state of the supply.' The expert who had come down to Calleshire to lecture to the force about drugs had taken a line from one of Shakespeare's sonnets as his text, 'Feeding on that which doth preserve the ill', but Sloan forbore to remind Detective Constable Crosby of this. Instead he said, 'And so it means some addicts will lose their wick without their usual fixes. Turn very nasty, some of them will if they're cut off from the stuff.'

The drugs expert had gone on a bit about fungible economies as well but Sloan had decided that while perishable goods consumed in use might well be a problem down Mexico way, they weren't in Calleshire.

'We could pick a few of 'em up now, sir,' suggested Crosby with something approaching animation. 'Before they turn nasty. There's that little runt, Goddard, who hangs about under the railway arches most nights . . .'

'Ah,' said Sloan with satisfaction, 'I knew I'd heard the name before. No, Crosby, he's only small fry. And so, in a way, is Horace Boller. The excise people have let him think they've accepted his story about not knowing what was in his lobster pot because it's the big fish we're after. He might even lead us to him,' he added without much hope.

'We could always arrest Wayne Goddard for possession with intent to supply, sir.'

'It wouldn't get us any nearer the people we really want.' They hadn't needed that expert on drugs to tell them this in Calleshire.

Crosby's face cleared. 'I get you, sir. You want us to sit back and see where any trouble from this missing consignment leads.'

'You've got it in three,' said Sloan unkindly. 'By the way, Crosby, if you had a vast amount of money in small denomination notes what would you do with it?'

The constable sounded quite reproachful. 'Buy a blue Jaguar XKR, sir, naturally.'

'Naturally.' Sloan sighed. 'Look, there's the road for the Greatorex.'

'So why are we going there, then, sir?' asked the constable, disappointed. Granary Row, where the Greatorex Museum was situated, was nowhere near far enough away from the centre of Berebury for his taste. Crosby liked long, fast journeys against the clock, or, better still, hot pursuits; not sedate progresses round the built-up parts of the market town at moderate speed.

'I think we could call it an ego trip,' murmured Sloan caustically. As far as he was concerned he would only be really interested if the mummy were stuffed full of heroin.

'If I had lots and lots of money, sir,' said Crosby, as they entered the museum car park, 'really lots, then I'd have one of those, too.' He pointed to a vintage green Bentley with polished coachwork and gleaming chrome headlamps. 'Just for show, of course.'

'Naturally,' said Sloan again. 'And a TVR Grantura for Sundays, I suppose.'

The curator of the museum, like Sloan, lost no time at all in categorizing the police visit as a sheer waste of time and public money. 'It's bureaucracy gone mad, Inspector,' declared Marcus Fixby-Smith heatedly. He turned to his deputy, a thin colourless woman, who flanked his desk. 'I've never heard such utter nonsense, have you, Hilary?'

Hilary Collins shook her head.

'I can assure you, Inspector,' said the curator, 'that every single piece of Colonel Caversham's legacy to the museum here is only of archaeological interest.'

'And archival,' put in his deputy in support. 'I'm afraid, though, we haven't had time to go through all of the written material yet, let alone begin to catalogue the collection. There's rather a lot of it.'

'The colonel's early travels are particularly well documented,' said Fixby-Smith. 'He was a pioneer in his day.'

'A true explorer,' said Hilary Collins reverently. 'They don't come like that any more.'

'Which is why we're so pleased to have this legacy of all the artefacts in his collection,' said Fixby-Smith. He gave Sloan a remarkably shrewd look. 'I promise you, Inspector, that it's got very little intrinsic value outside the museum world.'

Detective Inspector Sloan, who had been a policeman long enough to know that everything – but everything – had some value to someone, somewhere, duly made a note.

'Presumably,' went on Fixby-Smith, 'that's why he left it all to the Greatorex in the first place.'

'The family might have chucked it, you mean?' asked Detective Constable Crosby insouciantly.

'They might,' Fixby-Smith said, adding disparagingly, 'You never can tell with people who don't know the first thing about artefacts.'

'But the relations get the real money, do they?' enquired the detective constable.

The curator stiffened. 'I couldn't tell you who the residuary legatees are. We at the museum haven't been informed.'

'I don't think that's our concern anyway, at this

stage, sir.' In principle, Detective Inspector Sloan was all in favour of 'blue skies research' – finding out all you can before you begin an inquiry – but that was something that didn't seem to apply here.

Hilary Collins said diffidently, 'But surely, Inspector, we can do what the coroner wants and certify that the mummy is merely an ancient survival? After all, even if we don't know the exact provenance we do know that it's Egyptian.'

'I'm afraid, madam,' said Detective Inspector Sloan with genuine regret, 'that the coroner requires rather more than your formal certification.'

'Ancient isn't the right word anyway,' interrupted Marcus Fixby-Smith. 'Even without seeing any radiocarbon datings I am prepared to state on paper, on the basis of its style and condition alone, that the mummy in question is definitely in the region of three thousand years old. Isn't that good enough for the man?'

'What the coroner is asking for,' said Sloan, euphemistically paraphrasing as best he could as he went along, 'is the written opinion of a registered medical practitioner.'

'Then I only hope,' said Fixby-Smith acidly, 'that that practitioner has some idea of how much damage can be done to a mummy like this just by starting to open it up in the wrong way. I've been in touch with a palaeopathologist who's an acknowledged authority on the subject. Miles, that is, Professor Upton, advises me that the whole procedure calls for very great care.'

'I'll tell the doctor that,' promised Sloan. 'You must understand,' he hastened on, 'that we're not in any way doubting the professional expertise of either of you here.' Sloan looked from one curator to the other and said, 'But surely, at the moment, your opinion could be based only on a view of the outer coffin?'

'Yes, but no one's going inside it, no one at all,' Fixby-Smith started up again with vigour, 'doctor or not, until it's been properly X-rayed first. I hope that's clearly understood. And that whoever does the X-rays is familiar with radioactive isotope techniques.'

'I'll be sure to pass your message on to Dr Dabbe, sir.'

'Dr Dabbe?' said Fixby-Smith.

'He's the Consultant Forensic Pathologist to the Berebury and District Hospital Trust,' said Sloan.

'Then, perhaps,' suggested Miss Collins timidly, 'he might be able to tell us the cause of death of the mummy at the same time.'

Chapter Four

Stained

'I would be the first to agree, Sloan,' said Dr Dabbe, with whom the two policemen were discussing the problem, 'that the cause of death can often be determined in really old bodies.'

'Even after three thousand years, doctor?' asked Sloan. He and Detective Constable Crosby were sitting in the consultant pathologist's office at the hospital in Berebury.

'You can tell a lot about illness from some mummies,' said the doctor. He nodded in the direction of the mortuary beyond his office. 'More than you can from some modern bodies.'

'I don't see how that's possible, doctor.' Crosby was at his most mulish. As far as the police constable was concerned, being in the pathologist's office was better than being in the actual mortuary – but only just. 'Our doctor doesn't even know what's wrong with my granny's stomach and she's still around.'

'Ah, that's because mummies are dead before they're examined,' said the pathologist by way of professional solidarity. 'Easier to get at the evidence so to speak. The abdomen in the living is *terra incognita*. In the dead it's terra firma.'

The constable looked unconvinced.

'But,' continued Dabbe, 'it's only in theory, gentlemen, that you can tell a lot about mummies . . .'

'In theory, doctor?' Sloan hastened into speech before Crosby's grandmother's illness could come back into the exchange.

'In theory,' repeated the pathologist firmly. 'And that's only if we were to open up that mummy over at the museum and I was to examine the remains for you.'

'I rather think that is exactly what the coroner has in mind, doctor,' murmured Sloan; although he was actually still unsure about this. Finding out was very high on his agenda.

'Which, Sloan,' said Dr Dabbe amiably, 'is only because our Mr Locombe-Stableford does not as yet understand the risks involved.'

'Risks?' Detective Constable Crosby's head came up sharply as he showed real interest for the first time. 'Danger, you mean?'

The pathologist smiled gently. 'Precisely, Constable. Danger.'

'Who to?' asked Crosby immediately.

'You and me,' said the pathologist.

Crosby clearly didn't like the sound of that.

'And, of course,' added Dabbe largely, waving a hand around, 'to anyone else who might happen to be around when the mummy is unwrapped.'

Crosby liked the sound of this even less. 'But, doctor . . .'

'Without my taking a great many additional precautions, that is,' carried on Dr Dabbe. 'Such as those I've just had to apply to my last post-mortem examination.'

'What sort of danger?' enquired the constable curiously.

'From spiders that come in with banana boxes?' suggested Detective Inspector Sloan. A local supermarket had once seen fit to send for him urgently for one such on the pedantic grounds that it was a suspected illegal immigrant. That, in Sloan's book, hadn't been real police work.

'Disease,' said Dr Dabbe.

'You mean disease in the dead can harm us?' asked Crosby.

'It's called contagion and mummies can carry old diseases,' said Dabbe. He pointed in the direction of the door of the mortuary. 'And so, incidentally, can new bodies.'

Detective Constable Crosby looked unhappy.

'My last case, on the other hand,' went on the pathologist, unusually expansive, 'was a new body with a new disease and I still had to take plenty of preventative measures.'

Detective Inspector Sloan nodded his comprehension of this coded message. 'Aids?'

'In my opinion, yes. Mind you, one mustn't be judgemental . . .'

'No, doctor.' The fine difference between crime and sin was dinned early on into every new recruit to the police force.

'And I, Inspector, was taught that the true pathologist

should only be concerned with white and yellow fibrous tissue not moral fibre.'

'Yes, doctor.' It was when crime and sin overlapped that the policing became really difficult.

'Mind you, Sloan,' the doctor said, tongue in cheek, 'it's the yellow tissue that's elastic.'

Detective Inspector Sloan would have been the first to agree that moral fibre was elastic too, but he held his peace. Heroin, considered purely as a substance, was morally neutral. Possessing it wasn't legal. Supplying it to others was a crime of the first order. But that wasn't the pathologist's concern just now.

'I think it might have been more fast living and fast dying with that poor fellow in there,' said Dabbe. 'He was nothing but a living skeleton.'

'Not slow dying, then,' said Sloan, who had come across other victims of acquired immune deficiency syndrome. 'Rattling with pills . . .'

'I'm told that this man chose one last fling, expense no object, instead . . .' said Dr Dabbe.

'And who would blame him for that?' said Sloan.

'Makes the certification a bit difficult, though,' said Dabbe jovially. 'A two-horse race, you might say.'

'Two-horse, doctor?' The pale horse of the Apocalypse which was Death, Sloan knew about. He searched his memory for the other three – War, Pestilence, Famine.

'Aids and alcohol,' said Dabbe neatly. 'I think it was the strong drink that got him in the end. Not your problem, of course, Sloan, this poor fellow.'

'No, doctor.' One thing which life on the beat had

taught Sloan very early on was the great importance of not taking on matters which were not his problem. 'Now, about this mummy at the museum . . .'

'I think,' said the pathologist briskly, 'that the best course of action would be for me to get our medical imaging people to take one of their portable X-ray machines over there and take some pretty pictures of your mummy for Mr Locombe-Stableford.'

'That would be very helpful,' said Sloan. It would give him breathing space to think about where that consignment of heroin would have been going, had it come ashore at Edsway in the hands for which it had been intended.

Dr Dabbe stroked his chin. 'A bit of non-destructive testing should get things started nicely.'

'And that,' said Sloan, 'should keep the museum people happy, too.'

The doctor reached for a notepad. 'I'll have a word with Steve Meadows and ask him to get in touch.'

'Meadows . . . I don't know that name.'

'You wouldn't, Inspector. He's the slowest driver in Calleshire.'

Sloan refused to rise to this. 'And?'

'And he's our friendly neighbourhood radiologist, too.'

Detective Inspector Sloan nodded. 'An X-ray report should satisfy the coroner, all right.'

It wasn't one of his more accurate forecasts.

'I think,' said Marcus Fixby-Smith to Hilary Collins after the two policemen had gone on their way from the museum, 'that this little local difficulty over Colonel Caversham's bequest is something our Howard ought to know about, don't you?'

She nodded energetically.

'I'm sure, anyway,' said Fixby-Smith, 'that he would want to know that the police have been here.' They were standing in the institution's Roman Room where the curator was resting his elbows on a handy stone sarcophagus. 'Straight away, if not actually sooner.'

His assistant hastened to agree with him.

'After all, you might even argue,' drawled Fixby-Smith, 'that dealing with outside trouble is what the Chairman of the Museums and Amenities Committee is for.' Marcus Fixby-Smith could deal with inside trouble at the museum himself any day, but he was very strong on self-preservation in an outside world he perceived as naturally hostile to arts administrators.

If Hilary Collins saw any inherent contradiction between this statement and Fixby-Smith's frequent assertions that all the town council's committee chairmen were useless ornaments, she did not see fit to say so at this moment. Instead she said loyally, 'Good idea.'

'And I should say that dealing with something like this would be right up Howard Air's street, wouldn't you?' said Marcus.

Howard Air, a high-profile member of Berebury Town Council, was a successful businessman and local politician. And while he did not know anything about art – and never failed to say so – even Marcus Fixby-

Smith had to concede that the man did seem to know his way around.

Hilary nodded. 'I would.'

'Moreover,' he added cynically, 'if there's any public relations mileage to be had out of any of this, then he'll want to make the most of it. After all, he wrings every drop of goodwill out of his connections with the Lake Ryrie project.'

Howard Air was a prominent supporter of an animal rescue reserve in the Kingdom of Lasserta, as well as being associated with the local centre.

Hilary Collins contented herself with saying, 'Howard Air certainly wouldn't want to hear anything about the museum at second hand.' She personally supported a lion at the Lake Ryrie Reserve with a small monthly donation. A photograph of the magnificent beast stood on her desk where others had pictures of their spouses and children.

Fixby-Smith grimaced. 'My guess is that he'd reckon learning about trouble from anyone else was a networking failure.' Howard Air, as Marcus Fixby-Smith knew only too well, was not one to go in for failure. On the complete contrary, as the museum curator for one would have been the first to admit. His committee chairman had been singularly good at attracting new funding for the Greatorex Museum's various exhibitions, especially the experimental ones. It was this last that had really earned Howard Air the curator's respect.

Hilary Collins had let her gaze drift in the direction of a nearby Roman stele. 'I dare say he doesn't have too many disappointments in that line.'

Fixby-Smith lifted his elbows off the stone sarcophagus and straightened up. 'No, but even Philistines can't win them all, Hilary.'

'What do you mean, Marcus?' Her mind strayed again to the inscription on the stele: she really must find the time to take another look at it. The Romans in Calleshire would be an interesting subject for schools.

'He lost that little Chardin oil which I told him he ought to bid for. It was rather nice, I thought. It went to some gallery in France.' He grinned. 'I had thought any painting with oranges and apples ought to go down well on his office wall.'

Howard Air and Company Ltd were big importers of fruit and vegetables for the wholesale market which supplied the county of Calleshire.

'Pity,' said his assistant. 'He could have used it in his advertising.'

Fixby-Smith shot her a sharp glance. The thing about Hilary Collins was that you never knew whether she was joking or not.

Howard Air was actually talking about advertising at the time, but not of either his own business or the museum. He was over at the village of Edsway.

'I think we'll need some better posters soon, Alison. Got to keep a high profile for the Lake Ryrie Project. They need every penny we can send them.'

Alison Kirk looked despairingly round the ramshackle Calleshire Animal Sanctuary which she and her sister, Jennifer, ran in spite of great financial difficulties.

'Of course, Howard, I do understand.' She sighed. 'There's so much need everywhere . . .'

'But here in Calleshire,' he reminded her gently, 'there's no danger of any of your animal species becoming extinct.' A chorus of barking dogs in the background endorsed this. 'Now, out in Lasserta . . .'

'Of course.' She turned a tired face towards him. 'We had more trouble here last night, Howard. The police were very kind but . . .'

'The police?'

'Someone called them out. Two of the mares got out on to the road. It was our fences, Howard. They'll really have to be mended properly now if we're going to help horses here as well.'

Air frowned. 'We can't have that, can we? I'll have to see what I can do. We might be able to spare some wood.'

'Inspector Harpe told us the two of them caused havoc with the traffic on the Larking road. Jennifer went out to see if she could help and said that cars were backing right up to Billing Bridge.'

'No one hurt, I hope?' he asked throatily.

'Not this time. We may not be so lucky the next time it happens.' She turned away from him so that he couldn't see her face. 'Have you heard about our poor nephew?'

'Derek? No. What about him?'

'He died,' she said bleakly. 'It . . .' her voice faltered and then picked up again. 'It was not unexpected.'

*

46

'Oh, thank you, officer.' The radiographer who had arrived at the museum with Dr Steve Meadows was young and pretty. She smiled sweetly up at Detective Constable Crosby as he helped her align the portable X-ray machine with the side of the mummy case. 'You're very kind.'

Crosby beamed.

'Now,' she smiled again, 'if you would just lift that cable there for me . . .'

'This one?'

'Take care,' she said. 'It's very heavy.'

The constable squared his shoulders like a latter-day Hercules applying himself to one of his labours. 'Where do you want it putting, miss? By the coffin?'

'*Cartonnage,*' said Marcus Fixby-Smith snappily, making it quite clear that radiology was not the only expertise around in the museum and that he, too, knew a pretty young girl when he saw one.

'We'll start with the cranial area, please, Ruth,' called out Steve Meadows, the Berebury radiologist. He turned to Sloan. 'You can't tell how the anatomical remains are lying within the casket at this stage, Inspector. If we can establish the position of the naso-frontal suture, that should get us started.'

Getting finished and done with rather than getting started was what interested Sloan, but he did not say so.

'All the same,' carried on the radiologist chattily, 'I can't think what's got into the coroner. He's usually pretty reasonable.'

'Perhaps he's interested in ancient Egypt,' murmured

Sloan, at the same time noting that Crosby was getting increasingly interested in the petite and present-day young radiographer, who still managed to look attractive in spite of wearing a lead apron.

'Or just anything nubile,' said Meadows, almost equally *sotto voce*. 'Great place for beautiful girls, Nubia.'

'Perhaps,' contributed Marcus Fixby-Smith, who wasn't used to being left out of any conversational exchange going, 'the coroner thinks the ancient Egyptian practice of weighing the heart of the deceased against the Feather of Truth would be an improvement on an inquest.'

'Well, there's one good thing to be said for X-raying a mummy,' remarked the radiologist in more everyday tones.

'Really, doctor?' In Sloan's book there wasn't anything at all to be said for spending a whole morning on it when he was so busy with the drugs scene.

'It doesn't have any trouble keeping still when it has its photograph taken. That makes a nice change,' he added feelingly.

A line of verse from a Great War poem flitted through Sloan's mind: something about confusing stillness with death. It would come back to him presently.

'Now, officer,' Ruth, the radiographer, was saying prettily to Crosby, 'if you wouldn't mind just standing well back, please, while I take some pictures.'

The constable obediently moved away and commanded the mummy to say cheese as the X-ray machine started to make clicking noises.

Hilary Collins, the deputy curator of the museum,

said tentatively to Dr Meadows, 'I understand, doctor, that mummies usually have a gold plate over the embalmer's point of incision of the body. It would be most interesting to see that on an X-ray. Would it show up?'

'Indeed it would.' The radiologist was all affability. 'Metals – all dense materials, actually – look white on an X-ray film. Less dense ones go down through all the shades from grey to black.'

As far as Sloan was concerned most of the dense subjects with whom he usually came into contact were regrettably human. Their ethics also went down through the varying shades of grey. It didn't help that what the law itself wanted was a state where everything was either black or white.

The radiographer turned away from her machine for a few moments as she busied herself with a cassette of film, and then she asked Steve Meadows if he could step her way for a moment.

'I don't seem able to get a good picture somehow, doctor,' she said. 'It's coming up completely white.'

Steve Meadows looked down at something she was showing him and then up at Marcus Fixby-Smith. He asked, 'These old chaps didn't ever line their – what did you call them – *cartonnages* with lead, by any chance, did they?'

'No,' said the museum curator without hesitation. 'And, anyway, two men wouldn't have been able to lift this little lot if they had.'

'That's what I thought,' murmured the radiologist absently, still peering down. 'The preliminary radiograph's a bit odd, that's all.'

'Usually,' explained Marcus Fixby-Smith, one specialist to another, 'the body was just wrapped in a sort of cerecloth – a set of bandages made of the fibres of flax and so forth and often secured with a plant gum.'

Steve Meadows nodded.

'And sometimes, they applied resins to the outer wrappings as well. I'm not a specialist, of course. Egyptology isn't my field, by any means.'

'According to this plate,' said Meadows slowly, 'there's something else in there. Something metallic.'

'Gold?' suggested Hilary Collins. 'The Egyptians had plenty of gold.'

The radiologist glanced at Sloan and said, 'If Mr Fixby-Smith wouldn't mind indicating how to open this mummy, doing the least damage possible, then I think we may be able to tell you.'

'Good,' said Sloan heartily, as the curator and the radiologist advanced on the wooden casing, apparently oblivious of any of the dangers feared by Dr Dabbe. Time, after all, was getting on and Sloan had other work to do.

What wasn't good, though, was the noisome smell which assailed the nostrils of everyone in the room as the lid was prised open.

The metal inside was not gold. It was aluminium and looked suspiciously like domestic baking foil. It was wrapped carefully round something mummy-shaped. The odour got very much worse as Dr Meadows carefully unfolded a little corner and found not the nasofrontal suture of the skeleton he had been seeking but a partially decomposed body.

Chapter Five

Faded

'Of course there's a dead body in that mummy case,' said Superintendent Leeyes testily. 'You should have known that, Sloan. It's the whole idea of mummification.'

'Not an old body, sir,' said Sloan down the curator's telephone: he didn't think this conversation was for the open airwaves. He was alone in the curator's room. Marcus Fixby-Smith had turned a nasty shade of green when he had looked at the contents of the *cartonnage*, and had gone somewhere to be sick. Unexpectedly, Miss Collins had proved to be made of sterner stuff and was remaining with the hospital team and the opened case, holding a watching brief for the museum.

'Besides,' continued Leeyes, not listening, 'that's what the coroner's been making all this silly fuss about. You know that, too, Sloan.'

'A new body, sir.' If his message was as incomprehensible as Leeyes was finding it, then it might just as well be sent *en clair*.

'Not mummified remains?'

'No, sir.'

'How new a body?' he asked suspiciously.

'I think it could be described as nearly new, sir.' The words conjured up in his mind the shop on the corner of Nethergate called Secondhand Rose which specialized in nearly new clothes. 'But not very.' The recollection of the stench that had assaulted the olfactory organs of everyone in the gallery at the museum when the aluminium foil had first been peeled back made him catch his breath all over again. What was inside certainly hadn't smelled of roses of any sort.

Nor in any way, either.

'And what does that mean?' demanded Leeyes trenchantly.

'About a week old,' said Sloan. 'At least, that's what the radiologist – he's called Dr Meadows – puts it at, although he says the rate of decomposition of human bodies isn't his speciality. He told us,' Sloan consulted his notebook, 'that you have to be anosmic to be a good pathologist and he isn't.'

'Bully for him,' said Leeyes morosely.

'Yes, sir. I think it means not having any sense of smell.'

'Well.' He sniffed. 'I suppose you could say decomposing bodies are our speciality, Sloan, so you'd better get your skates on and find out who he or she . . .'

'She.'

'She is.'

'Was,' amended Sloan. 'She's very dead.'

'And,' continued Leeyes, undeterred, 'work out who put her there.'

'Yes, sir. And exactly why they put her there, too, of course.' The word that had come first to his mind about the setting was bizarre, but that didn't mean there wasn't a reason for using the mummy case.

'If you ask me,' said the superintendent, never one to be interested in the rationale of things, 'people always make too much fuss about the whys and wherefores of crime.' He sniffed again. 'Especially defence counsel. They make out that motive's the be-all and end-all of felony and it isn't, Sloan. Remember that.'

'No, sir. I mean yes, sir.'

'They'll say anything in mitigation, some of 'em,' he grumbled. 'Anything at all.'

'Yes, indeed.' Sloan toyed with the idea of mentioning that sometimes, where crime was concerned, if you knew the reason why it had been perpetrated, then you knew who had done it; but he decided against doing any such thing. His superior officer would doubtless mount yet another hobby horse if he did and there just wasn't time for that now.

'However,' continued Leeyes, 'you'd better get on to finding out what gives pretty quickly, Sloan, because a new body in an old mummy is something that the press'll be on to before you can say Granville Locombe-Stableford.'

Sloan tightened his lips. It was Granville Locombe-Stableford whom he wanted to talk to most of all. How and why the coroner had come to take an interest in this particular Egyptian mummy was the greatest mystery of all.

'So get moving, man.'

Sloan, who didn't need any assistance in imagining the probable headlines in the tabloid newspapers, merely said, 'Dr Dabbe's on his way over here now, sir, to see the body *in situ* before it goes over to the mortuary.' Marcus Fixby-Smith's office and its telephone were at a safe distance from the mummy but he would have to go back to the body as soon as the pathologist arrived. He wasn't looking forward to sharing the available air of the room with the stinking corpse again. He took a deep breath and said, 'The Scenes of Crime people'll be here soon, too, sir; although I don't think the museum was the scene of the actual crime.'

'And then,' said Leeyes, who was at a safe distance from any unpleasant sights and smells, 'you'd better start looking into where old Colonel Caversham came into this.'

'If he did,' murmured Sloan.

'Explorer, wasn't he? And Egyptologist.'

'Yes, sir. I've made arrangements to see his executors. He died months and months ago though, and the house has been empty since.'

'Trust the lawyers to take their time about winding up his estate.' Leeyes took off at yet another tangent. 'Half a year or more seems par for the course.'

'But as the mummy came from the colonel's house only yesterday,' Sloan promised hastily, before the superintendent could launch into yet another diatribe against the legal profession, 'we're going to examine it as quickly as possible. I've put a man on guard until we can get over there.'

'You can get up to a lot of no-good in an empty house,' rumbled on Leeyes. 'A happy hunting ground . . .'

'And as soon as we get some information about the

body – teeth and so forth – we'll try to get on with a positive identification.' Sloan glanced down at his notebook again. 'All the radiologist would say was that he thought the woman would have been in her early to middle twenties and very much on the small side.'

'I suppose you could say that narrows the field,' observed the superintendent unfairly, 'but not a lot.'

'And,' went on Sloan tonelessly, 'Dr Meadows also said that in his opinion the cause of death was not natural.'

'Presumably,' said Leeyes silkily, 'he has grounds for making that judgement.'

'In spades,' murmured Sloan under his breath. Aloud he said, 'Dr Meadows diagnosed a fractured skull.' He coughed and added, 'And that is his speciality.'

'The heirs of Colonel Caversham?' Simon Puckle sat well back in his chair in the offices of Puckle, Puckle and Nunnery in Berebury. This distancing served to emphasize further still the intimidating expanse of green leather desktop which lay between himself and the two detectives sitting in front of him. The desk was absolutely bare save for one sheet of paper.

'Or the keys of Whimbrel House,' said Sloan flatly. 'Whichever is the quicker.'

'The keys you may have now, Inspector,' returned the solicitor courteously. 'I'm afraid that producing the heirs of Colonel Caversham may take a little longer.'

Sloan's head came up on the instant. 'How come?'

'We can't find them,' said Simon Puckle.

'Not nowhere?' intervened Detective Constable Crosby, leaning forward.

'Not yet,' responded the solicitor obliquely. 'And it's not for want of trying.'

'Where there's a will there's a way,' said the constable sententiously. 'And a relative.'

'You've advertised?' said Sloan.

'Until we're blue in the face, Inspector,' said Puckle. 'Or in the red at the Calleshire County Bank's executors' account, whichever way you care to look at it.'

'But items have already been sent to the Greatorex Museum . . .' began Sloan. This was true, if unspecific.

'That is, Inspector, we haven't yet been able to trace the immediate heirs of the colonel's settled estate – the residuary legatees. Most of that part of the inheritance goes to his male heirs-at-law under an old family trust.'

'But not until you find them,' contributed Crosby intelligently.

'Precisely, Constable. I may say that handing over the specified non-pecuniary legacies has posed us – that is Puckle, Puckle and Nunnery acting in their capacity as the executors – no problems as yet.'

'I see, sir.' Detective Inspector Sloan decided, for the time being, against informing the solicitor of the problems already posed by one particular bequest. That could wait.

'The famous Caversham collection of antiquities has gone to the Greatorex Museum in Berebury,' enumerated Puckle, 'and the colonel's library was sent to Almstone College at the University of Calleshire last week. As you may imagine, that was extensive and specialized – and valuable, of course.'

Detective Inspector Sloan nodded.

'And,' continued Simon Puckle, 'the original manuscript of his noted work on Ra'fan in Upper Egypt went to the Society of Calleshire Archaeologists, of which Colonel Caversham was president for so long.'

'So . . .' began Detective Inspector Sloan.

'And then,' swept on Puckle, 'there were a few bequests to his favourite charities: his regimental association, the Calleshire Animal Sanctuary – he'd been a cavalryman in his time and remained very attached to horses – and the parish church at Staple St James. They're having trouble with their steeple, you know.'

'Really, sir?' Trouble with church steeples was happily outside his remit; and, he reminded himself feelingly, sometimes it seemed it was about the only trouble in 'F' Division that was. 'These heirs . . .'

'Not heirs general of the body,' amplified Puckle. 'Just the son or sons or grandsons of the colonel's younger brother's son.'

Crosby screwed his face up in thought. 'His nephew's family?'

'That's right.' Simon Puckle nodded. 'I'm afraid that in the old colonel's eyes the nephew was the black sheep of the family.'

Crosby brightened. 'A no-good boyo?'

'Not really,' said the lawyer, recipient of countless family secrets. 'Not by today's standards, anyway. The colonel belonged to an earlier age and just didn't see things the way we do now.'

'What did the nephew do, then?' asked Crosby with interest. 'Run off with the family silver?'

'Ran off with someone else's treasure,' said Puckle drily. 'Their daughter. It was a long time ago, of course.'

'Which made it worse,' agreed Sloan, who sometimes felt he was getting behind the times himself. Marriage, it seemed to him, had come to resemble more and more a game of musical chairs: a change of place – or none – every time the music stopped.

'My grandfather,' said the solicitor, himself the fifth generation in the legal firm, 'told me that the girl's family had had high hopes of an alliance for their daughter with a young sprig of the Ornums at the time when she went off with the Caversham boy.'

That explained the opprobium to Sloan's mind. Marriage to the younger son of an earl carried an irreproachable cachet, whoever the Cavershams of Staple St James might have been.

'The Dorothy Vernon touch, you might say,' murmured Puckle.

'Sir?' said Sloan.

'A distinguished elopement from Haddon Hall in Derbyshire in the sixteenth century,' explained Puckle. 'Dorothy Vernon was an heiress who ran away with her lover during a ball.'

Sloan nodded. The sixteenth century might have been a world without prohibited drugs but it was before the Married Women's Property Act.

'Made for a blot on the Caversham family escutcheon though, I'll bet,' remarked Crosby.

'They married and disappeared abroad,' said Puckle

repressively. 'Neither was ever heard from by the colonel again.'

Crosby hummed the tune of 'After the Ball was Over' under his breath.

Puckle coughed. 'Gerald Caversham resigned his commission, of course.'

'Of course,' said Sloan, although he was not quite sure why a love match – let alone marriage – should have rendered Gerald Caversham unfit for military service.

'If alive,' rejoined Puckle, 'he'd be in his early seventies by now but . . .' He paused.

'But . . .' prompted Sloan gently.

'I have to say – and I have had to say this to the ultimate heir – that we are getting increasingly doubtful that he is.'

'So he got cut off without a shilling, did he?' asked Crosby. 'The no-good boyo, I mean.'

'No, he didn't. And the colonel couldn't have done that even if he'd wanted to,' said Puckle. 'The settled estate was entailed . . .'

'Come again?' said Crosby.

Detective Inspector Sloan sighed heavily and hoped that he wasn't the one who was going to have to explain to Crosby about the fruit of the loins.

Simon Puckle explained that this entail meant that the colonel's property had to go to the male heirs of the body male and to no one else, the laws of primogeniture still applying.

Detective Constable Crosby said that sounded all very unfair to him.

The solicitor, with distinct echoes of Mae West and goodness, said that fairness had got nothing to do with it. 'But, remember, the colonel was still a reasonably wealthy bachelor. One supposes,' Puckle added mildly, 'that this is how he was able to enjoy as many expeditions abroad as he wanted.'

'Quite,' said Sloan. His own wistful ambition, when young, had been to explore the Matto Grosso in search of Colonel Fawcett's body. Sloan, though, had never been wealthy, and had not stayed long a bachelor. 'And if the immediate heirs can't be found?' he asked, conscious that time was passing.

'Should that be the case, and it can be demonstrated beyond doubt that neither Gerald Caversham nor his sons . . .'

'If he had had any,' put in Crosby, who gave every appearance of still following the narrative closely.

'If he or they had had any,' agreed Puckle, 'and had not left male issue, then the entire Caversham inheritance reverts to the descendants of a remote collateral relative called Peter Caversham who is presently living in Luston.'

He made Luston sound like one of the Cities of the Plain rather than a prosperous industrial town at the other end of Calleshire.

'Who you say is aware of this?' said Sloan.

'Very well aware,' said Puckle drily, 'even though the colonel tried to have it kept from him.'

'So if we might have the keys of Whimbrel House from you as executors . . .' said Detective Inspector

60

Sloan, conscious that he had already sent a man to guard the building.

'Because getting a search warrant takes time,' added Detective Constable Crosby quite gratuitously.

Chapter Six

Marked

Marcus Fixby-Smith, curator, led the way into his office at the museum.

'Sorry dragging you over here like this, Howard.'

He paused at the threshold of the room, conscious as always on these occasions of the perennial dilemma of deciding where to sit in the presence of the Chairman of the Museums and Amenities Committee. If he sat behind his desk he automatically put his chairman, older and more senior, in the supplicant's chair on the other side. If he offered his own seat to Howard Air, he himself felt displaced and ill at ease.

'Don't worry, Marcus. I get my work done while everyone else is in bed.' Howard Air gave a deprecating cough and solved Fixby-Smith's little local difficulty over protocol by perching on the radiator under the window. Where the curator was flamboyant and given to gesture, the fruit importer was compact and controlled. 'It's all over in the market for the day by your breakfast time.'

Fixby-Smith sank thankfully into his chair. 'Naturally,' he said, 'the police won't tell us anything more at this stage.'

'Naturally.' Howard Air cocked his head forward, listening attentively to the museum curator. 'Go on.'

'Before they took it away, all that they would do was confirm that the *cartonnage* contained the decomposing body of an unknown female.'

'Which you knew already,' pointed out the committee chairman.

'Too right.' Fixby-Smith gave a convulsive shudder. 'But only after it was opened up. I didn't know before, of course.'

'Of course not. Pull yourself together, man. Nobody will think you did.'

Fixby-Smith gave no sign of having heard him. 'And now,' he swallowed visibly, 'the police want to know everything there is to know about Colonel Caversham's legacy to the Greatorex.'

'I'm not surprised,' said Howard Air. The businessman might not have known much about art but he was a lot stronger on common sense. 'It's only what you would expect, surely?'

'But I can't tell them anything except that all the bequest was brought over from Staple St James by Wetherspoons yesterday.'

'Then you'll have to tell them that, won't you?' Because the man was sitting in the window and with his back to the light, Fixby-Smith could not see his face properly. 'It shouldn't be too difficult. The museum's legacy was quite straightforward, wasn't it? Surely it's only the residuary estate that's got 'em all tied up in knots?'

The curator jerkily pushed some learned journals

about on his desk and squeaked, 'How was I to know that Colonel Caversham'd gone and left us a dead body?'

'He didn't,' said Howard Air reasonably. 'He left us some mummified remains, which he'd had for years and years at Whimbrel House in a mummy case which you had seen there before. If what you say is correct, whatever's in there now was put there long after the colonel died.' He looked suddenly serious. 'Like last week . . .'

'We've had a look in the ottoman and that great Ali Baba jar he was so proud of and even in the pithoi. Silly, I know.'

'You're not thinking straight, Marcus.'

'It's all very well for you, Howard,' said Fixby-Smith, emboldened by the circumstances, 'but you didn't see that body and I did. It was all wrapped up just like an oven turkey.'

Howard Air sat in silence for a moment, deep in thought. 'It's a funny business, all the same.'

'I just can't get it out of my mind.'

'The other funny business is exactly how the police came into it,' said Air as if Fixby-Smith hadn't spoken. 'Something odd must have happened to make them take an interest in the first place.'

'We didn't send for the police, Howard.'

Howard Air looked up quickly. 'That's what I mean.'

'I just can't fathom it.'

'Who else knew the museum had been left this collection of the colonel's?'

Marcus Fixby-Smith pushed his floppy hair back away from his eyes. 'I couldn't say. His solicitors, of course, and the removal people, naturally, and I suppose the other legatees whoever they may be.'

'And your staff here.'

'Of course,' said the curator stiffly. 'But we hadn't made any public announcement yet. If you remember, we planned to make a bit of a public relations splash about the colonel's entire collection coming to us, but only after it was put on display so that the public could come and see it for themselves.' He gave a hollow groan. 'God, Howard, we'll be making a splash all right and no mistake, as soon as the newspapers get to know about this.'

'It'll hit the headlines, I dare say.' The chairman sounded more resigned than particularly perturbed at this. 'So, our announcement will have to be different, that's all.'

'You must be joking.'

'You have to ride with the punches in life, Marcus, you know.' He regarded the museum curator quizzically and decided against proceeding with this line of thought. 'Look, we'll have to have something prepared for the sake of the museum, so we'd better get to work on it straight away.' He pulled a piece of paper out of his pocket. 'Come along.'

Marcus Fixby-Smith didn't respond to this. 'Howard, the police asked if we knew of any missing persons.'

'And do we?' asked Howard Air, his pen held at the ready.

'Only Rodoheptah,' said the museum man, true to his calling. He gave a high uncertain laugh. 'We don't know where he is, do we? Not now.'

Howard Air stopped, his pen suspended in mid-air. 'I hadn't thought of that,' he said seriously.

'You've got a problem with a fractured skull, Seedy, have you?' echoed his old friend, Inspector Harpe, from Traffic Division. 'Well, funnily enough, we've got a problem with a fractured skull, too.'

'Tell me,' invited Sloan. He had joined the man from traffic at his table in the police station canteen and was trying to snatch some food while the body was being brought over to the mortuary in Berebury.

'Remember that bloke who was hit in his car over at the Larking crossroads over towards Edsway? Name of Barton, David Barton. Well, he's got one, too. A bad one.'

'But that was weeks and weeks ago...' Sloan's problem fractured skull was much worse than bad but he let his friend have his say.

'Six weeks,' said Inspector Harpe succinctly.

'So?' asked Sloan cautiously. He wondered what was coming next since Inspector Harpe's pessimism was legendary. The officer was known throughout the Calleshire force as 'Happy Harry' on account of his never having been seen to smile. Inspector Harpe, for his part, always maintained that there was never anything in Traffic Division at which to so much as twitch the corners of the lips. 'How come he's still traffic's problem?'

'Still unconscious, that's why.' Harpe shrugged his shoulders. 'His wife thinks he's beginning to respond to her voice but the people at the hospital aren't as optimistic as she is.'

'I dare say they're being pretty careful not to raise false hopes.'

'If you ask me, the doctors there don't believe he's ever going to come round.' Harpe sank his fork into a sausage. 'I'm coming to believe that the Larking and Edsway junction is jinxed.'

'Bad driving,' said Sloan briskly.

'Crossroads were sacred in pagan times,' said the traffic man. 'Didn't you know that?'

'Don't you start, Harry. I've had enough of the ancient past already this morning.'

Harpe ignored him. 'And after that,' he said, 'they hung felons there and then buried them on the spot. No wonder the place is spooked.'

'If it isn't bad driving,' asserted Sloan firmly, 'then it's driving under the influence of drink or drugs.' He was aware that his own anger at the invasion of the countryside, his countryside, by drug dealers was irrational, but he couldn't be doing with superstition either. Not in this day and age. 'There isn't anything else left, Harry.'

Inspector Harpe speared another sausage.

'Drugs cause a lot of accidents,' went on Sloan earnestly. It wasn't the only damage they caused, he reminded himself. That was the trouble. There was no end to the criminal consequences of drug dealing. And now all he could do was to sit back and wait to learn the consequences of a dearth of heroin. For all he knew, the absence of heroin could be worse than its presence.

'You'll have to watch it, Seedy,' advised his old friend. 'You've got drugs on the brain these days.'

'We always knew that they were coming in through Kinnisport,' said Sloan, 'and now we can prove it, but that's all. Customs and Excise pick up what they can but they can't stop all the traffic. No way.' He looked curiously at his old friend. 'Harry, if you had more hard cash in small denominations than you could account for, what would you do with it?'

'Put it in the bank,' said Inspector Harpe promptly. 'They could count it, too.'

'No good. The banks have a legal duty to inform the regulatory authorities.'

'Pay off my mortgage, then,' said Inspector Harpe. 'And buy a bigger and better house.'

Sloan shook his head.

'No good?' said Harry.

'No. The conveyancing solicitor could rat on you – should rat on you, come to that – if you couldn't show the dibs had been come by honestly.'

'New car? I've always wanted a Rolls-Royce Silver Cloud myself.'

'A man can only have so many new cars without the neighbours talking.'

'Ours even notice if we have a late night,' conceded Harpe. 'The stock market?'

'Your name goes on the register of shareholders.'

'Difficult.' Harpe screwed up his face. 'Could I take it abroad?'

'You could try,' said Sloan. 'A lot of drug dealers do.'

'I'd change it into francs or guilders or something. Big notes, of course.'

'Smurfing.'

'Are you having me on, Seedy?'

'No. That's called smurfing.'

'Sounds like it's from a kid's comic.'

'Nothing funny about it. It goes on all the time. We've been watching that Bureau de Change down by the station for yonks.'

'No joy?'

'Not yet.'

'It wasn't drugs at that crossroads.' Harry came back to his own field. 'It was drink. The blood alcohol was way over the limit in the driver who hit that poor fellow Barton, but he's the one who's in hospital still dead to the world. He was lucky not to be T-boned.'

Detective Inspector Sloan sipped his mug of tea. 'He doesn't sound to have been all that lucky to me.'

'His wife says that his employers are going spare without him,' said Harpe. 'He's a senior audit clerk with Pearson, Worrow and Gisby, you see . . .'

'The accountants?' Sloan knew Jim Pearson for a busy man but one still with time to lend a hand with good causes.

Harpe nodded. 'Mrs Barton says they don't know which way to turn, they're so busy. Apparently, her husband's a real workhorse and accountants need work-horses. Mind you, Seedy,' he added with unconscious brutality, 'all we're doing is holding our horses. We've charged the guy who hit Barton with driving under the influence. Just to be going on with, mind you.'

'You can't do a lot more with everything hanging in the balance,' agreed Sloan, aware that Harpe's difficulty was a procedural one. 'At least your problem is still alive. Mine's too dead for my liking.'

'Talking about holding our horses,' went on Harpe, undiverted.

'Yes?'

'We had trouble over at Edsway last night with real horses.' The faintest glimmer of what might have been a smile crossed his features. 'Had to hold them ourselves.'

Sloan cocked a professional ear. 'My sort of trouble or yours?'

'A couple of mares got out of the animal sanctuary over there and created merry hell with motorized traffic on the road to Larking.'

'Horses and cars don't mix,' said Sloan profoundly, echoing, had he but known it, the sentiments held by that old horse soldier, Colonel Caversham.

'They'll have to mend their fences at the sanctuary,' growled Harpe, pushing his plate away, 'or they'll have more trouble.'

'Only literally,' said Sloan neatly. Alison and Jennifer Kirk had more friends and supporters in Calleshire than most people. The Sloans' own cat, Squeak, had come from the Calleshire Animal Sanctuary as a rescued kitten. Sloan pushed his chair back. 'Well, Harry, I hope your driver survives.'

'Talking of surviving,' riposted Harpe unkindly, 'I'm

surprised that that young driver of yours hasn't come to grief yet.'

'Crosby?'

'Him.'

'Luck, I expect,' said Sloan mordantly.

'Or the devil looking after his own,' said Inspector Harpe, still determinedly superstitious.

'Fractured skull, Dr Meadows says, does he, Inspector?' Dr Dabbe shot a quizzical glance in the direction of the door leading from his office to the mortuary. 'Well, Steve should know, shouldn't he, Ruth?'

The radiographer, who was clutching some X-ray photographs under her arm, nodded energetically. Detective Inspector Sloan was standing, his notebook at the ready, while Burns, the pathologist's perennially silent assistant, was hovering between office and mortuary in the manner of an old-fashioned butler. They were all gowned and masked, and had been offered the opportunity of opting out of being present at the post-mortem in case remnants of dangerous diseases were still lurking in the mummy case. None of them had, although Detective Constable Crosby had removed himself to the furthest corner of the room.

'And, of course,' said Dr Dabbe genially, 'there's a very famous precedent.'

'There is?' Detective Inspector Sloan pulled himself together and tried to take a proper interest in the past.

'In the year 1352 BC, give or take a year.'

'Really, doctor?' The pathologist was as bad as Happy

Harry. Sloan didn't like to say – not yet – that it was the present that was so very pressing.

'Tutankhamun, too, so it is said, Sloan, received a fatal blow to the back of the skull . . .'

'Did he, doctor?' The original occupant of the mummy case might have been Egyptian but the present one wasn't.

'In a place on the cranium where an accident is most unlikely.'

'We'd call that suspicious circumstances, all right,' conceded Sloan, his mind still on the here and now but keeping the police end up withal.

'Probably while he was asleep, or at any rate lying down,' said the pathologist. 'Upon his secure hour, as Shakespeare put it so well. I've always found the murder of Hamlet's father very interesting, Sloan. That ear poison . . .'

'Some other time, doctor, please,' pleaded Sloan. 'Some other time.'

'Right.' He picked up a hand microphone and started dictating into it the fact that in view of the nature of the subject of the examination, all present had consented to be present and were clad in their extra-special precautions outfits.

'Dr Meadows thought you might like some straight X-rays *in situ*, Dr Dabbe,' said Ruth, a trifle shakily. 'And I could do some A and P ones for you now but not an encephalogram, of course.'

'A and P?' queried Sloan quickly. He had a rooted objection to being excluded from the shorthand of other people's trades and professions. Jargon for in-groups –

a badge of belonging – was what it was and he didn't like it.

'Anterior and posterior, Inspector,' replied Ruth.

'Full frontal,' interpreted Dr Dabbe cheerfully.

'That's if the foil could be opened up a bit more,' the radiographer said, wincing.

'Your pretty pictures would be very helpful,' said the pathologist gallantly. 'We're going to need X-rays sooner or later.'

Detective Inspector Sloan hoped that the radiographer was not a militant feminist.

'And you, Inspector,' went on Dr Dabbe courteously, 'I take it you already have all the photographs you need of the – er – *cartonnage?*'

Sloan nodded as Burns advanced with a trolley laid out with instruments.

'I suppose,' said Dr Dabbe in a businesslike way, 'that you'll be wanting a time frame first, Sloan.'

What Detective Inspector Sloan wanted first was the chance to get started on the hunting of the coroner's nark, but he did not say so.

Chapter Seven

Frayed

'I am given to understand, sir,' said Detective Constable Crosby to the young man on the doorstep, 'that last week you reported a woman as missing from this address; that is, if you're Colin Thornhill.'

'Jill Carter,' said the young man tightly. 'Have you found her?'

'Not yet,' said Crosby.

'So why have you come round here?'

'Just checking, sir. That's all.'

'Not again!' protested Colin Thornhill heatedly. 'Do you realize that you're the third policeman to want to ask me questions since Jill went missing?'

'Am I, sir?' asked Detective Constable Crosby. He was standing on the doorstep of a big old house opposite the park in the middle of Berebury. 'Well, I never.'

'There was the one when I reported that Jill hadn't come home last Friday . . .'

'That would be our Station Sergeant,' offered Crosby helpfully.

'And then another policeman came round here to ask me the same questions all over again. And now you.'

Colin Thornhill stood back from the threshold and said grudgingly, 'I suppose you'd better come in then.'

He led the way up to the top flat of a house that had come down in the world. Where once a successful Victorian merchant had proclaimed his worldly achievement in architectural curlicues, now half a dozen souls made their individual homes. The apartment under the roof into which Thornhill showed the constable had clearly begun life as a set of night nurseries.

'Jill disappeared, you see,' the man said, 'without a word to anyone. Just didn't come home that night.'

'There's no law against disappearing,' said Crosby.

'I understand that.' He essayed a thin smile. 'I've been tempted to do it myself often enough when things haven't gone well, but Jill just isn't that sort of person.'

'If you want to drop out, then you can,' said Crosby. This was a credo oft-repeated to the families and friends of those who had done so by those who moved in police circles. The families and friends invariably remained unconvinced of this truism. 'There's nothing to stop you or anyone else going off if you want to without saying why.'

'Jill wasn't a drop-out,' Thornhill came back at him swiftly, exhibiting the first sign of animation that he had seen so far.

'No?'

'No,' he said firmly. 'Besides, she'd just started a new job.'

The constable looked down at the report in his hand. 'As a trainee with Pearson, Worrow and Gisby, the chartered accountants.'

He nodded. 'It was beginning at the bottom, of course . . .'

Crosby nodded. So was detective constable.

'But it was a foot on the ladder.'

So was the office of detective constable.

'And,' he said wanly, 'we hoped it might lead somewhere.'

'Naturally, sir.' Where Crosby wanted his career to lead was straight to Traffic Division.

'My own employment being in the nature of things uncertain.'

Crosby glanced down again at his notes. 'Actor?'

'When I get the chance, or even half a chance.'

Detective Constable Crosby, being still young himself, probably understood the scenario better than his seniors: boy meets girl who is in work when he isn't; girl meets boy in need of support and gives it. Colin Thornhill was probably a sort of caveman in reverse.

'But Jill hasn't been back to the office either,' Thornhill was saying. 'That's what's so very worrying.' He hesitated. 'They weren't best pleased about that; what with her being new and them being so busy just now.'

'Overworked, was she?'

'No.' He shook his head with an instant understanding. 'It wasn't like that at all, officer. Jill just isn't the sort to consider suicide. I'm sure about that. Quite sure,' he added with emphasis. 'I can't see her having a nervous breakdown.'

'Good,' said Detective Constable Crosby with a wholly artificial enthusiasm; it wasn't suicide that the police were worrying about. Women with skulls fractured by a heavy blow on the sinciput did not then proceed to immolate themselves in mummy cases in empty houses.

'Oh, she was working hard enough, all right,' Thornhill went on, 'because the firm was very short-staffed. But the actual work wasn't too much for her or anything like that. She said the more she did, the more interesting she found it.'

'And how long ago did you last see her?'

'I haven't set eyes on her for nearly a week now,' he said dully, lapsing back into his previous weariness of manner, 'and neither has anyone else.'

'And where were you when you did?' Crosby had been taught that quite a lot of police work amounted to asking questions to which he would already know the answer. The importance of the procedure lay in the way in which the answer was given the sixth or seventh time round, and in particular whether or not the response was exactly the same as it had been the first and second time the question had been put. Most experienced police officers held that way to be better than any number of lie detectors.

'The Ornum Arms at Almstone,' said Thornhill, naturally oblivious of this train of thought. 'It makes a nice walk. We'd just been having a drink together there after she'd finished work on Friday.'

'And she left?'

'And I left, not her. She stayed on at the pub. She said she'd spotted someone she knew who she wanted to talk to.'

'A friend?'

'She didn't say.'

'Who was it?'

'Search me,' said Thornhill. 'No, hang on. I heard her call him Nigel as she went over but I didn't know him. So I made myself scarce.'

'You did, did you?' said Crosby, projecting considerable scepticism. 'I'd like a description of this man, please. And then?'

'Then I went to do a bit of shopping on my way home. You see, Jill didn't like shopping.'

'But you'd had this row . . .'

'We hadn't had a row.' He flared up instantly. 'That's not true.'

Crosby looked down at the report in his hand again. 'Over some curtains.'

'Who told you that?' he challenged him.

'I couldn't say.'

'But all Jill and I had been doing,' he said carefully as if repeating something he had said again and again, 'was discussing what colour our new curtains should be.'

'A row,' repeated Crosby.

'That wasn't a row,' he said with scorn. 'That was a normal domestic talk-through.'

'Domestic?' The word had overtones at the police station.

'We've been together for quite a time,' Thornhill said with seeming irrelevance.

'Then what?' asked Crosby.

'She just didn't come back here after that.' He leaned forward and sank his head between his hands.

'And?' Crosby discounted the gesture. The man could be a trained tragedian.

'When it got very late I rang the Ornum Arms. Johnny Hedger – that's the landlord – said she wasn't there but he couldn't remember when she'd left.' He pulled his lips up in the travesty of a smile. 'I expect that's what all landlords always say to women who telephone asking for their men.'

'Could be.'

'Well, I can assure you that they do it when men ring up asking for their women now, too.'

'Very possibly, sir.'

'And then I rang the hospital in case she'd had an accident.'

Crosby glanced down at the report. 'We checked that, too. Routine.'

Colin Thornhill pulled himself up and, giving Crosby a very direct look, said, 'What did you come here for if you've got it all written down as you obviously have?'

Crosby shuffled his feet, his eyes cast obliquely. 'The name of her dentist, please.'

The great importance of body language and its correct interpretation had been one of the features of the detective constable's training. He had also been taught those elements of it which can be counterfeited. Crosby was well aware, too, that the man to whom he was now talking was a professional actor and thus likely to have his facial responses under control.

But he knew of no way in which even the most accomplished thespian in the world could cause the blood to desert his own face in one fell swoop, or bring about a sudden visible burst of perspiration to the temples.

It was evening by the time Detective Inspector Sloan and Detective Constable Crosby got to the Ornum Arms at Almstone. Even from the outside of the public house it was apparent that the hostelry was full to overflowing.

'Looks like they're having a party, sir,' said Crosby as he manoeuvred the police car around the crowded car park. 'Parking's a bit tight.'

'If you scratch this or any other vehicle here,' observed Sloan dispassionately, 'they'll never have you in Traffic Division.'

'Sounds like they're having a party, too,' said Crosby, affecting not to have heard him. A door had opened as the two policemen walked towards the entrance to the pub and noise was spilling out all over the car park for all the world like molten metal. Out of the door slid a slight figure who quickly made his way out of the nimbus of light.

'Wayne Goddard,' said Crosby. 'Shouldn't have thought it was like him to leave a party early.'

'He's either seen us coming,' said Sloan, 'or sold out of whatever he's selling. Come on, Crosby. Let's get inside before anyone else slinks away.'

. The decibels were even higher inside the building. Johnny Hedger, the brawny licensee, and two barmaids were all pulling pints of beer as fast as they could. Good landlord that he was, Hedger wasn't too busy to notice the arrival of the newcomers. He waved a hand in greeting and then applied himself again to serving his queueing customers. When the press at the bar had abated a little he raised the counter flap and slipped out from behind the beer handles to join them.

'Evening, gentlemen,' he began warily. 'Come to join the party, then? All welcome, of course. Derek said so.'

'Derek?' enquired Sloan, looking round. 'Derek who?'

'Oh, Derek's not here,' said Johnny Hedger. 'Couldn't very well be in the circumstances, could he?'

'Oh? Why not?'

'Because poor Derek's dead, of course.'

'Like poor Fred,' murmured Sloan half under his breath.

'Poor Fred?' The landlord looked quite bewildered.

'Forget it. So poor Derek's dead, too, is he?' asked Sloan. The landlord's words had just caused him to be revisited by a schoolroom memory. 'Fred's dead' was a fragment of English history that had stuck in his mind, like Queen Anne being dead, too. Queen Anne's death had made less impression on him, though, than that of the son of George II who, had he not been poor Fred and dead, would have been George III instead – or rather, Frederick I.

Sloan had sometimes wondered if an essay he had once been made to write at school on the natural, and unnatural, propensity of the eldest sons of the monarch not to come to the throne was what had first led his own footsteps in the direction of the police force; inheritance and crime so often being almost inextricably intertwined. He'd called the essay 'Uneasy lies the head that's meant to wear the crown' and been quite pleased with himself.

'And Derek didn't want anyone to go to his funeral,' Johnny Hedger was explaining. 'Anyone at all. Not even his aunts.' Johnny looked meaningfully in the direction of a small table by a window where two older women were sitting slightly apart from the throng. 'Perhaps,' he added thoughtfully, 'especially not them.'

'The Kirk sisters,' said Sloan, noting automatically that most of those in the bar were relatively young and male. Jennifer and Alison Kirk looked oddly out of place among the others. 'From Edsway.'

'All Derek wanted,' insisted Hedger, 'was a big party for everyone here the day after he died. Not comfortable words mumbled over his grave that he couldn't hear anyway.'

Detective Constable Crosby looked round at the crowd of drinkers. 'For a wake, you could say it was going full swing.'

The festive atmosphere was enhanced by the boatman, Horace Boller, who was sitting within easy reach of the bar, cradling a large tankard in his horny hands. For once there was a positively benign expression on his leathery old face.

The landlord pointed to the shelf behind the bar. 'There's a lot of money sitting there for tonight, I can tell you.'

'Beauty is in the eye of the beer-holder,' remarked Crosby to no one in particular.

'A whip-round?' asked Sloan, ignoring this.

Hedger shook his head. 'No. That would have been

chicken feed compared with what's behind those bottles. There's proper money there, Inspector. Plenty of it. Derek gave it to me a couple of months ago against today.' He pointed to a jeroboam standing on the counter. 'And he stuffed a lot of fifty-pound notes into that for the Lake Ryrie Reserve too.' He stared at the enormous bottle. 'It's usually five-pence pieces that go in there.'

'So he knew he was dying, then.'

'We all did,' said the publican solemnly. 'He'd got one of those illnesses that the insurance companies call dread.'

'People forget that not all diseases are curable,' observed Sloan moderately.

'Derek wasn't going to get better from this one,' said Hedger briefly. 'And he knew it.'

'When you gotta go, you gotta go,' contributed Crosby.

'Derek said that he was going to enjoy what was left of his life,' said the publican. 'And who could blame him for that?'

'No one,' said Sloan. Every man had to treat his personal rendezvous with death at its disputed barricade in his own way.

'As it happens, there wasn't a lot of life left for him after that, either.' Hedger sighed. 'I lost a good customer when Derek went.'

'Big spender?' asked Sloan with unconscious cynicism.

'Not really. Not in the ordinary way, but then not long ago, he got his hands on a lot of money.'

'After he'd been told that he was going to snuff it?' put in Crosby.

'Could be,' said Hedger, while Detective Inspector Sloan made a mental note. A working policeman was, perforce, always interested in anyone who had large sums of money to fling around.

Dead or alive.

The landlord suddenly straightened up and became mine host, asking what he could bring the two of them.

'Sorry, Johnny,' said Sloan. 'We're here on business.'

'Who's done what now, Inspector?' he asked, conspicuously unalarmed.

'Been seen here at the Ornum Arms and nowhere else since,' Sloan said succinctly. 'Last Friday, a week ago today. As to who . . .'

'Ah, that girl. Yes.' He frowned. 'I didn't see the going of her, I'm afraid. I remember the chap who came with her leaving on his own but she stayed on because someone she knew came in and I noticed him give her a little wave.'

'Any idea who that was?'

'Oh, I know him,' said Hedger. 'He's one of our local residents. Name of Worrow. Nigel Worrow. Lives in a biggish house near the shore. I can tell you one thing, though.'

'Yes?'

'The girl and the first man had had a bit of an up-and-a-downer before he left.'

'You saw that, did you?'

'Well, no, to be honest. I didn't myself but another customer – someone I'd never seen in here before –

told me about it. He'd been sitting in an alcove near them and he came over and sat near the bar instead. Told me he couldn't stand domestic arguments; that was why he had come to the Ornum Arms in the first place. To get away from them.'

Detective Inspector Sloan decided not to say anything about the occasions when people who had arguments in public houses rather than private ones needed constabulary assistance to break them up. Usually late on Saturday nights.

'You'd think two people could find something more important to have a row about than new curtains, wouldn't you?' said the innkeeper, too calm a man himself to argue with anyone.

'I'm not so sure about that, Johnny.' He was aware that the words spoken that morning *chez* Sloan about roses had been harsher than they should have been.

'Perhaps you're right,' said the landlord sapiently. 'After all, Gilbert and Sullivan broke up over a carpet, didn't they?'

Sloan hadn't known the nature of that particular *casus belli* but he could believe it.

'Hang on, Inspector,' carried on Hedger, 'I've told one of your men all this already.'

'Just checking, that's all,' said Sloan.

'What I want to know,' said Detective Inspector Sloan without preamble, 'is exactly how the coroner got to know about this mummy being moved to the museum.' He had sent for Police Constable Douglas Stuart, a man almost too portly for any duty calling for really hard physical activity, first thing the next morning.

'Ah,' said Doug Stuart, the coroner's officer.

That, Sloan reminded him swiftly, did not constitute an answer.

'No, sir. I agree, but . . .

One of the more agreeable fantasies which Detective Inspector C. D. Sloan entertained in his mind from time to time was that of being invited to write a testimonial for Police Constable Douglas Stuart in the happy event of his needing one for a different job. Sloan had it ready and waiting in his imagination. 'Anyone,' he would write, 'who gets Douglas Stuart to work for him will be lucky.'

' . . . we didn't know then that it was only a mummy, sir,' mumbled Stuart.

'Ah,' said Sloan unfairly.

'We thought it was a proper body, you see. One that had been moved without the coroner's say-so.'

'And what were your precise grounds for entertaining this misapprehension about the coroner's permission?' asked Sloan frostily.

'There was a letter that came. No, not a letter, more of a note. Done on a word processor, we thought.'

'To the coroner?'

'It came through the door of his office but it wasn't addressed to anyone . . .'

'And well covered with the fingerprints of other people by now, I'll be bound,' interrupted Sloan.

' . . . asking if we knew that a body had been improperly removed from Whimbrel House at Staple St James.'

'I shall need to see that letter.'

'Yes, sir.' Stuart made as if to rise and thus escape this interrogation.

'Anything strike you about it?' said Sloan before the man could lumber to his feet.

'There was no address on it, and it was unsigned, sir.'

'Then what?'

'Then I first checked with Morton's, the undertakers, sir, and they said that they had buried Colonel Caversham from that address months ago but they hadn't been to the house since.'

'And Whimbrel House? Did you check that?'

'Several times, sir. Silent as the grave. No one there at all. So Mr Locombe-Stableford said he was going to take the matter up with the superintendent. He did do that, sir, didn't he?' asked Stuart anxiously. 'Like he said.'

'He did,' said Sloan shortly.

'Then we heard a whisper on the grapevine that all the fuss had been about an old Egyptian mummy after all.'

'Only in a manner of speaking,' said Sloan.

'And then we realized that someone was having us on. I'm very sorry, sir.'

'No, Stuart,' said Sloan, 'they weren't.' He took a deep breath. 'It isn't your fault. They were having us on, not you.'

Chapter Eight

Scuffed

'But what I want to know, Sloan,' declared Superintendent Leeyes testily, 'is exactly who is having who – that is whom – on.' The superintendent had recently attended an evening class on English grammar and was now inclined to pedantry.

'And why,' added Sloan.

'I must say I don't get it myself, Sloan.' He sniffed. 'All this playing about with typed anonymous notes being sent to the coroner. Indeterminate paper without fingerprints, you say.'

'Yes, sir. Talking about fingerprints, sir . . .'

The superintendent was undiverted from his train of thought. 'Why didn't whoever wrote that letter send it to us instead? Tell me that, Sloan. We get loads of anonymous letters here at the station and I don't suppose the coroner gets many at all.'

'Perhaps that's why it went to him, sir. Whoever wrote it might have been afraid it could be overlooked in the pile here. Or not followed up quickly enough for their purposes, whatever they happened to be. We don't know that yet, either.' He took a deep breath. 'Talking about fingerprints, sir . . .'

'Well?'

'Crosby took some prints from the furniture in the flat of a young woman who was reported as having gone missing last week. Name of Jill Carter, of Park Drive, Berebury.'

'And?'

'Dr Dabbe got some from the body in the mummy case.'

'Snap?' he growled.

'Yes, sir,' said Sloan soberly. 'I'm afraid they were what you might call a matching set.'

The superintendent leant back in his chair and waved his pen in the air. 'So we can now say that there is one known fact in an uncertain and very murky world.'

'Yes, sir,' Sloan assented without enthusiasm. 'We know the name of the body in the mummy case.'

'The identification of the deceased is something to be going on with, whichever way you look at it, Sloan.'

'True, sir.' Sloan agreed with him even though 'Confusion worse confounded' was the sentiment that was actually going through his mind. 'The only other thing we have at this moment is the knowledge that someone wanted us to find her.' Somewhere in his memory was a quotation about what someone didn't know wasn't knowledge, but it was proving strangely elusive.

The superintendent frowned. 'It's not a lot, is it?'

'No, sir.'

'But if that particular someone wanted us to find the body,' said Leeyes, 'why did they go to the trouble of parking her in that mummy case? Must have taken a lot of effort.'

'I think, sir, it can only be because that someone wanted to control exactly when the story broke.'

Leeyes grunted. 'Myself, I would have thought that putting her under some bushes in the park would have done just as well. People are always poking about in the park.' He brightened. 'She might even have been written off as having gone for a lark in the park in the dark. You never know. That's happened before now. Saved someone a lot of effort.'

'I don't think so, sir,' Sloan said repressively. 'She worked for those accountants in River Street. I'm seeing them next.' Something his friend Harry Harpe had said came into his mind. 'Now I come to think of it, they were already short-handed before Jill Carter went missing.'

'As bad as solicitors, accountants.'

'I think she was put where she was and the letter sent to the coroner to control exactly where she was found as well as when,' spelt out Sloan. 'So both must be important.' That, too, was something to be going on with. 'It's a question of where we should begin.'

There was a certain Peter Caversham of Luston to be seen as well: a man waiting in the wings, with a vested interest in nobody else turning up to claim the Caversham inheritance.

Leeyes cheered up. 'You've got the boyfriend, though, haven't you?'

'We know where Thornhill is,' said Sloan cautiously. 'And statements have been taken.'

'More than once, I hope.'

'Yes, sir.' It was common knowledge in the Force that the superintendent, too, subscribed to the dictum in *The Hunting of the Snark*: 'What I tell you three times is true.'

'And, Sloan, don't let one murder divert you from this drug smuggling business. Drugs kill more people every day than murderers.'

'I won't forget, sir. Actually, it did occur to me that Horace Boller might have been using the animal rescue place at Edsway for his own purposes.'

'I wouldn't put anything past him.'

'It would make a good pick-up point for supplies of heroin,' said Sloan, thinking aloud. 'You could hide anything over there.' He made a note. 'We'll take a proper look as soon as we get half a moment.'

'Just here, Crosby,' commanded Detective Inspector Sloan from the passenger seat, 'will do nicely, thank you.'

There is one respect in particular in which police officers differ from the generality of men and women. This is in the matter of their right to park their vehicles at the kerbside in working hours in crowded roads. River Street, Berebury, where Detective Constable Crosby brought the police car to a standstill in the middle of the morning, was one of the market town's busiest commercial thoroughfares.

He drew up outside one of the stylish old houses which were a reminder of the prosperous waterborne trade of former times. Where once merchants had lived in some splendour, offices now held sway. Those of

Pearson, Worrow and Gisby, Chartered Accountants, were workaday in appearance but by no means in bad order.

Sloan enquired of the receptionist if Mr Pearson would see him. The girl picked up a telephone. 'That you, Jim?' she asked with a notable lack of formality. 'Cheryl here. An Inspector Sloan would like a word.'

A door at the far end of the corridor opened and Jim Pearson ushered someone out of a room. Against the light as that someone was, it took Sloan only a moment or two to make out the short stocky outline of Howard Air, a long-time member of the local magistrates' bench. Howard Air recognized Sloan immediately, although his usual punctilious greeting of the policemen was somewhat muted.

'Terrible business at the museum, Inspector,' he said. 'Terrible. Even worse for Jim here, of course, because he knew the poor girl. At least Marcus Fixby-Smith didn't, although he's still in a pretty poor state. Didn't sleep at all last night.'

Jim Pearson, seeming much older than the last time Sloan had seen him, looked as if he, too, had had a sleepless night. 'First David Barton with his life hanging by a thread for weeks and weeks, and now Jill Carter dead.' He sounded dazed. 'I can't believe it.'

'Barton is a victim of a road traffic accident,' said Sloan, remembering his chat with Inspector Harpe. He added tautly, 'Jill Carter has been murdered.'

'Yes, yes, I know, Inspector,' the accountant protested, 'but they are both people.'

'So,' said Sloan, before Pearson could move on to

John Donne's sonorous 'any man's death diminishes me', 'I'm afraid we are going to have to take statements from you and your staff.'

'Then I'll be taking my leave, Jim,' murmured Howard Air, looking older and greyer, too, than when Sloan had last seen him. He moved towards the outer door and, waving a farewell at Sloan and Crosby, said huskily to Pearson, 'Thanks for all your help, Jim.'

Inspector Sloan watched the businessman go and then said casually to the accountant, 'Is Mr Howard Air one of your clients, then?'

Jim Pearson smiled ruefully. 'I only wish he was. His company must be about the biggest in Berebury.' He jerked his thumb in the direction of the other side of the river. 'No, it's our upmarket rivals over the way who benefit from auditing the accounts of Messrs Air and Air, Fruit Importers Limited.'

'So . . .' Sloan knew which firm he meant. Ickham and Grove were at the very top of the local league of accountants, and knew it. They were also quite concerned that everyone else in the county of Calleshire knew it, too.

'So you want to know what Howard Air was doing here?' Pearson relaxed a fraction. 'That's easy, Inspector. We handle the financial affairs of the animal rescue outfit over at Edsway.'

'The Kirk sisters.'

'And their offshoot in Lasserta, the Lake Ryrie Reserve. All done for love, I may say. Howard's their patron, and it's no secret that he's a very generous one, too. They're lucky to have him do it, but I'm told he's a softie for anything on four legs.'

Sloan, who hadn't forgotten that Colonel Caversham had had a weak spot for quadrupeds too – equine ones, anyway – got back to the business on hand. He said, 'My constable here will be taking statements from all your partners and staff here with especial reference to the last time they saw Jill Carter alive.'

He would look into Howard Air's connections later. In his book and at this moment anyone who was involved with the Calleshire animal rescue set-up was worth a second look, just in case there was more in Horace Boller's baskets of fish than fish.

Something else worth a closer examination was the ownership of the beautiful old Bentley sitting outside the museum. When they were finished here at the accountants, Crosby could make quite sure that the classic car belonged to one of the few men in Calleshire whom he knew could easily afford it: Howard Air.

And if not him, then he could find out who.

'And I,' said Detective Inspector Sloan, 'would like to talk to the partners myself.'

This meant Nigel Worrow, since the only Gisby in the firm now was a callow youth called Kenneth who was still struggling with his examinations. Sloan gave every appearance of accepting this last information at its face value. He saw no need to remind anyone at the accountants that it was quite often callow youths who murder young girls, especially if the affections of those young girls are patently engaged elsewhere with rival suitors.

Nigel Worrow contrived to be courteous, brisk and solemn all at the same time. Like Jim Pearson he also looked tired and worried.

'A very sad business indeed, Inspector. We've never ever had anything like this happen in the firm before. Jill seemed such a pleasant girl – a good worker, too, and heaven knows, we need one. We're desperately short-staffed, what with our senior audit clerk having been out of action for so long. Did Jim tell you? His life's still hanging by a thread after all these weeks and poor Jill had been doing some of his work.'

Something in this caught Detective Constable Crosby's wayward attention. He said from the sidelines, 'And now you haven't got Jill Carter either.'

'Quite so,' said Worrow, visibly clamping his jaws together. 'Quite.'

'So when did you last see her?' Sloan hastened into more official-sounding phrases. The work that the dead girl had been doing would need to be looked at by someone to whom accounts were not a closed book, but not at this minute.

'Last Friday,' said Nigel Worrow.

'The day she disappeared,' observed Crosby.

'As it would seem, yes.' Worrow appeared unperturbed. 'I happened to drop into the Ornum Arms on my way home to Edsway and she was there with a young fellow. He looked as if he was on the point of leaving as I arrived.'

'Do you go there often?' asked Sloan, conscious of a certain triteness.

'Only on Fridays, Inspector. Johnny Hedger's an old

client; and,' he gave a tired smile, 'sometimes actually reaching the end of another working week seems to merit celebrating.'

'Did you speak to her?'

'Just in passing. The man she was with really did go just after I spotted her.'

'Had they been having a row?' asked Crosby.

Worrow looked surprised. 'Not that I saw or heard.'

'Would you be able to describe what she was wearing, sir?' enquired Sloan.

Here, Nigel Worrow revealed himself as the unobservant male, *par excellence*. He said he couldn't, but thought vaguely that she might have been wearing something green. And, yes, he had gone straight home to his wife and supper as usual after he'd left the Ornum Arms. The weekend he'd spent on his boat, sailing off Kinnisport. Also as usual, he added before Sloan asked.

'By the way,' said Sloan as the two policemen were leaving at the end of what had turned into a protracted enquiry session at Pearson, Worrow and Gisby, 'did your firm happen to act for the late Colonel Caversham of Whimbrel House?'

'We did indeed,' said Nigel Worrow without hesitation. 'For years and years.'

'And that included,' chimed in his partner, 'keeping any creditors happy while he was poking about in Egypt for months at a time.'

'What about the extended family?' asked Sloan, casually. 'Peter, for instance?'

Jim Pearson's face changed, his expression becoming

suddenly wary. 'Oh, you know Peter Caversham, do you? Yes, as it happens, we act for him, too.'

'Some clients don't like using their local firms,' supplemented Nigel Worrow.

'Too close for comfort?' suggested Crosby.

'The colonel was a decent old boy,' interrupted Worrow swiftly, 'except that he never did come to grips with inflation. Thought an old half-crown could still buy you most things.'

'The generation gap, you might call that,' said Jim Pearson, smiling weakly.

'I'm afraid, Inspector,' said Simon Puckle, 'that neither Fixby-Smith nor I worried about not leaving fingerprints on anything when we were here yesterday.'

The solicitor had decided that his responsibilities as executor and trustee required him to be present when Sloan and Crosby eventually reached Whimbrel House. Or, decided Sloan, it might have just been simple curiosity. After all, lawyers are only human, too.

'Our forensic people will take care of that,' murmured Sloan absently. 'They'll be asking you to give us your prints presently.'

'And Sid Wetherspoon and that young lad he had with him, I suppose,' said Puckle. 'They must have handled absolutely everything.'

'Them, too,' agreed Sloan. He didn't think it necessary to mention that the police probably had Wayne Goddard's fingerprints on file already. 'Who else has had the keys since the colonel died?'

The policeman on guard duty outside had already indicated to Sloan that there were no very obvious signs of breaking and entering about the house. The Scenes of Crime people would make absolutely sure. They were on their way now with the police photographers. Sloan was still debating in his mind whether or not Whimbrel House had actually been the scene of the crime. It would be for forensic science to establish if there were traces of blood on this or any carpet in the house.

'Only Sid Wetherspoon,' Simon Puckle was saying. 'He collected them on Tuesday so he could see which size of van he would need and make sure that there wasn't anything here that they couldn't handle.'

'Right,' said Sloan, hoping that there wasn't going to be anything about the murder of Jill Carter that the police couldn't handle. 'What about Peter Caversham? Was he ever here much as a young man?'

'As a boy, probably,' said Puckle, 'but not since. Latterly the colonel insisted that he could only come in the house over his dead body.'

'Like that, was it?' Detective Inspector Sloan automatically put an interview with Peter Caversham even higher on his list of priorities.

Detective Constable Crosby stirred. 'Didn't like the idea of it going to him?'

'Didn't like the idea of dying either,' said the solicitor.

'One of those who thought the world would come to a dead stop when he did?' said Sloan, who had met plenty of people like that. It was a concept that accounted for a lot of short-termism in public and private affairs.

'If our clients only appreciated,' said Simon Puckle feelingly, 'that they, too, were going to die, they'd make a will sooner rather than later.'

'And where there's death there's hope,' remarked Crosby to nobody in particular.

Detective Inspector Sloan sniffed, very much aware that the house had that curious smell of a building that had been empty for too long.

The solicitor must have sensed the same airlessness. 'What this place needs are some open windows.'

'Not yet,' Detective Inspector Sloan said. 'That will have to wait. Now, Mr Puckle, if you would just stay here in the hall, my constable and I need a proper look over the building.'

Whimbrel House at Staple St James, too, had been built in the more spacious days of yesteryear. Then, large families and dependent relations and the live-in servants to care for them all had called for many rooms. On the other hand, this ancient retired cavalry officer and explorer had clearly had his being in his study, an old army-style camp bed in the corner serving him as a bedroom *à la* Duke of Wellington in his last days at Walmer Castle.

Most of the rest of the furniture had gone, making the task of the two policemen easier. It was a simple matter to look first through empty attics, and then the bedrooms where once the ladies of the household had dressed for dinner. The fine drawing room and even finer dining room were similarly devoid of anything in the nature of goods or chattels and even the study, scene of most of the activities of Sid Wetherspoon and

Wayne Goddard, only had the scattered remnants of packing materials in it.

'Should have tidied up before they went,' muttered Crosby, opening the door of a butler's pantry and shutting it again after he saw it was completely bare.

'Somebody tidied something away, Crosby,' said Sloan astringently, 'and we've got to find it, wherever it is.'

In the event it was Detective Constable Crosby who did. He opened the door of a broom cupboard in the lobby of the great kitchen and jumped swiftly back as a bound and bandaged figure toppled forward to the stone floor at his feet.

'Dr Rodotheptah, I presume,' said Detective Inspector Sloan. 'Stand well back, Crosby, and don't touch. Remember, Dr Dabbe says such men are dangerous.'

Chapter Nine

Loose

'Don't touch the mummy, Sloan,' ordered Superintendent Leeyes equally swiftly; but for different reasons.

'No, sir.'

'And notify the coroner before you do anything else at all.'

'Yes, sir.'

'He isn't going to catch us out twice.'

'No, sir.' He decided it was no use trying to explain to the superintendent that Mr Locombe-Stableford hadn't actually caught the police out the first time; or that Her Majesty's Coroner for East Calleshire had patently been manipulated just as the police had been by some person or persons unknown – and both from motives that were still obscure to Sloan.

'And neither is anyone else, Sloan,' growled the superintendent. 'Remember that.'

'Yes, sir.'

'All the same, it seems to me,' Leeyes pronounced weightily, 'that someone somewhere is having a very good try at catching us out a second time.'

Sloan didn't attempt to deny this. He simply said, 'We're going over to see the boyfriend next.'

'Quite right, Sloan.' The superintendent was a great believer in the fact that murders were usually family affairs.

'And,' went on Sloan, well aware of this, 'we're trying to get a lead on a man called Peter Caversham, in Luston.'

'Don't forget to see Jill Carter's employer again, too,' Leeyes reminded him. 'The one who was the last person to say he'd seen the girl alive. Nigel Worrow.'

'I won't forget,' promised Sloan. 'There could well be something funny going on at his place.' As far as he was concerned, accounts could cover a multitude of sins any day of the week. Even the Calleshire Constabulary's own income and expenditure accounts listed buns and bribery under one single heading so that no one ever knew exactly how much was really spent on informers. The last person to query this had very swiftly been reminded how Sir John Falstaff had got it in the neck for his 'but one half-pennyworth of bread to this intolerable deal of sack!' and been sent on his way no wiser.

The superintendent was still speaking. 'Surely the colonel's house over at Stable St James isn't all that far from The Ornum Arms, as the crow flies?'

'No, sir,' replied Sloan, 'it isn't, but no one saw anything in the pub car park the night the girl went missing. Crosby checked.'

'Doesn't mean a thing.' His superior officer sniffed. 'Negative evidence in both senses.'

'Yes, sir,' agreed Sloan, since this was true.

Leeyes grunted. 'As I remember too, Sloan, Whimbrel House is a bit on its own, isn't it?'

'Quite isolated, sir.'

'Then they were lucky not to have had squatters in there, seeing it was empty for so long.'

What Sloan wanted to check was that they hadn't had drug distributors in there. Large, empty and isolated houses were ideal for the calculated division of big consignments of heroin into smaller, marketable amounts; and as he would have been the first to agree with the man from Customs and Excise, this work had to be done somewhere. And safe houses were hard to come by these days. He wondered how they had got to hear about it.

If they had.

'By the way, Sloan,' said Leeyes, 'you might make sure in passing that the coroner's officer does his share of the work.'

'Certainly, sir,' promised Detective Inspector Sloan with alacrity, as he put the telephone down. He turned to Detective Constable Crosby and said, 'There's one more call I want to make and then we can get going.'

The resources of the Calleshire Constabulary extended well beyond the county's boundary. They included instant access to specialists in matters far removed from the usual run-of-the-mill policing. The expert to whom Detective Inspector Sloan was now speaking was attached to a famous Fraud Squad, where she enjoyed the role of forensic accountant.

'Do call me Jenny,' she said.

'Yes, miss,' said Detective Inspector Sloan automatically. He must pull himself together. Somehow, he'd expected forensic accounting to be man's work. He was getting out of touch.

'And what exactly is it – er – Inspector, that you want to know about money-laundering by drug dealers?' She had a deliciously deep voice with a suspicion of a gurgle in it. 'Tell me . . .'

'I'd like some background, please, miss . . .' If she was expecting him to tell her his own Christian name she would be disappointed.

'Oh, Jenny, please.'

'Jenny.' He swallowed and started again. 'I'd like some background, particularly on the sort of scam we should be looking out for here in Calleshire where we know we have heroin coming in and dealers operating.' He must remember, too, that money-launderers as well as accountants could be female. After all, traditionally, women had always washed everything else, hadn't they?

A very feminine little laugh came trilling down the telephone line. 'Oh, it won't be a scam that you should be looking for, Inspector. Not if they really know what they're doing, that is.'

'Really?'

'What your money-launderer wants more than anything,' said the delicious voice, 'is for all his financial transactions to look absolutely straightforward and above board.'

'Yes, mi– Jenny.' She, of course, was speaking as if all wrongdoers were male. 'I can understand that but what . . .'

'You see,' she explained, 'your bad boy has only got two choices about what to do with all his ill-gotten gains: hide them or legitimize them.'

'If he hides them,' said Sloan vigorously, 'we'll never find them. That's for sure.'

'If he hides them then there's very little point in his having acquired them,' she who was called Jenny came back smartly. 'He might as well have not taken all the risks.'

'So he attempts to legitimize them,' conceded Sloan. That surely let Horace Boller off the hook; he wouldn't know how. Probably foreign to his nature, too.

'Which is when his danger moment comes,' said the forensic accountant, wise in her generation. 'So your money-launderer tries to do it in stages and in ways that don't leave an audit trail. Or, better still, he arranges to pay tax on the money. Nothing authenticates assets quicker than that.'

'Money talks,' said Sloan obstinately.

'But it can say different things when it does,' she said, adding sweetly, 'And it doesn't have to shout.'

He wanted to say something about it being the singer not the song that mattered to his Criminal Investigation Department but she was still talking.

'In our experience, Inspector, one of the favourite conduits in the first instance for this sort of money is classic cars.'

'Classic cars can be sold on fairly easily,' agreed Sloan, the vision of a certain beautiful green Bentley coming into his mind.

'So can most items bought in the fine art market,' the girl said.

'And no questions asked,' said Sloan. He was sure she was only a girl. She sounded quite young – and as pretty as a picture herself, fine art notwithstanding.

'It's more a case,' she said, 'that there will usually be no questions asked about where the money came from to buy the articles in the first place rather than in the second.'

'That's their danger point, is it?' The green Bentley would have to be accounted for, that was for sure.

'And then there is always smurfing – thanks to crooked Bureaux de Change.'

'They were the first places we looked,' Sloan hastened to tell her. 'Especially one near the station here that we thought might be dicey, but we found no great numbers of small sterling notes being converted into high denomination notes in other currencies.'

'And,' she sighed, 'some solicitors and accountants report nothing even when they should – such as large sums going to offshore accounts. Overseas connections are what your money-launderer likes. The more the better.'

Sloan still didn't see where the Lake Ryrie Reserve in Lasserta could come in. If it did. He wanted Jenny to go on talking though.

'Banks and building societies are much better at telling us about suspicious transactions,' she said, 'than accountants and solicitors are.'

'I expect it's because they tend to have a closer relationship with their clients,' said Sloan solemnly, suppressing any facetious suggestions about there being honour among thieves. Hc'd seen case-hardened solicitors in court give their clients the convincing impression they really cared that they had lost their clients' cause. 'The personal touch.'

'Could be,' said Jenny cheerfully. 'You might keep an eye open, though, for another popular way of using up a lot of cash in one fell swoop.'

'What's that?'

'Finding someone who owns something that's quite legitimate – a winning sweepstake ticket or an endowment insurance policy – and offering them over the odds for it. That sort of thing. Money's no object in drug-dealing circles, remember. They're not like the forces of law and order; they've got infinite resources. Make ours look like chicken-feed.'

'I suppose funds aren't a problem,' said Sloan, 'when you're rich beyond the dreams of avarice.' He didn't know who it was who had first said that but he did know who had said the love of money was the root of all evil. His churchgoing mother often quoted St Paul: 'It's quite a difficult concept – being too rich.'

The accountant's voice sounded suddenly quite sultry. 'Drug dealing is like having the Midas touch twenty times over.'

'That must have its dangers,' he said, prosaically.

'And, Inspector, don't forget that a money-laundering method founded on trust between drug dealers – word of mouth – is the hardest of all to trace.'

'Nothing in writing would be safer all round,' he

agreed. It was the so-called gentlemen's agreements that caused most trouble in the business world, though.

'They like the anonymity, too.' She gave another of her merry little laughs. 'It has its advantages for us though.'

'It does?' He couldn't match the accountant's detachment. He'd noticed that working with figures all the time did that to people. They lost interest in the human race.

'If there should happen to be a breach of that trust between any of your money-launderers, then you won't have to worry, Inspector.'

'They get taken out?'

'They do. There's justice among thieves as well as honour. But it's pretty rough.'

Sloan wondered for a fleeting moment if poor Jill Carter had overstepped the mark somewhere along the line, but the forensic accountant was still speaking in her attractive gurgle.

'What you have to remember most of all, Inspector, is that diamonds are still the money-launderers' best friend.'

The only aspect of life about the top apartment in the house in Park Drive, Berebury, which had changed since Detective Constable Crosby had last been there was the mien of its occupant, Colin Thornhill.

Now the whole physical bearing of the man projected total dejection and lassitude. Even police questioning had failed to arouse him. He was sitting at the table, his shoulders hunched up and his head sunk low between them. And the act of raising his head to respond to Sloan's calculatedly low-key interrogation appeared to call for more physical strength than he could conjure up.

Of emotional strength, Thornhill appeared to have none left at all. The answers he gave Sloan were monosyllabic and almost those of an automaton.

'No,' he repeated as often as the question was put to him, not moving his sunken head from between his hands. 'I've told you time and again that I haven't seen Jill since that day at the Ornum Arms, and that's the truth. Yes,' he insisted in the same low monotone. 'We were very happy together. Very.'

The only questions which did seem to stir him were about the row over the curtains. Probings there roused him very quickly. 'Whoever told you that, Inspector, got it wrong. We were only talking about them. Not arguing. Hell, what does the colour of curtains matter, anyway?'

Detective Constable Crosby, bachelor, nodded his agreement and murmured something to his superior officer about 'a domestic'. Detective Inspector Sloan was not quite ready to agree to this: by the same token William Shakespeare's *Othello* could possibly be dismissed as a fuss over a handkerchief.

And it wasn't.

'No,' said Thornhill dully to Sloan's next question. 'Jill hadn't mentioned this guy Nigel Worrow much. He was one of her bosses, but they were all brother and Bob and Christian names at her work. To listen to her you couldn't tell who was a partner and who was the caretaker. It didn't mean a thing. They just thought it gave a more friendly image to accounts.'

'More trendy, too,' contributed Crosby, who had always resented paying lip-service to those higher up the police hierarchy.

Detective Inspector Sloan said nothing but he did make a note. In the police book there was being friendly and being too friendly; more especially where pretty young women were concerned.

'Never heard of him,' said Thornhill in response to the casual trawling of Colonel Caversham's name across the conversation.

Interviewing an actor was not the easiest of undertakings. The uncontrolled, unpremeditated reaction was the one Sloan wanted, but actors were trained to tailor their physical responses and expressions exactly to the emotions they wished to exhibit. What Sloan wanted was the spontaneous and unguarded bounce back. He didn't get it.

'Or him either,' said Thornhill, when Marcus Fixby-Smith's name was mentioned. 'Who are these guys when they're at home, anyway?'

Sloan ignored Thornhill's riposte and carried on with his questioning.

'No, Inspector,' said Thornhill wearily for the fourth time, 'I do not know of any reason at all why Jill should have been murdered. And it doesn't matter how many times you ask me, I still don't know.' He then added with a complete absence of histrionics, 'I do know that nothing matters now. Nothing at all, whatever you say. I've lost the only person who mattered.'

The only time Colin Thornhill moved from his classic mourning position was when the interview was ending. He tottered to his feet like an old man, presenting an image far, far removed from the nimble athletic stage figure of before.

'I can tell you people one thing for free,' he said in a chillingly controlled way, 'and that's if I find either of those two guys you mentioned – Caversham or Fixby-Smith – had anything to do with murdering my poor Jill then they'll have me to deal with, too.'

'Customs and Excise, Kinnisport,' boomed the voice down the telephone. 'Jenkins here. How can I help you, Inspector?'

'Just checking.' Sloan began his litany: 'There's a man called Nigel Worrow . . .'

'The *Berebury Belle*,' said Jenkins promptly.

'Pardon?'

'The *Berebury Belle* is the name of his yacht.'

'Oh, is it?' Sloan paused for thought.

'Nice boat. Very trim.'

'Yes,' he said slowly. 'I can see that it might be.'

'Meant to be named after his wife, or so he says when asked.'

'You know it then?' asked Sloan. He didn't know whether Jill Carter had been pretty – a Berebury Belle too – or not. He thought she had been much loved but that was something different. Quite different. And sometimes even more dangerous.

'We know nearly all the yacht club craft,' said Jenkins with due professional modesty.

'Anything known about the man?' asked Sloan more specifically.

'Not exactly known,' said the customs officer cagily. 'But . . .'

'But?'

'But we've been keeping an eye.'

'With good reason?'

'He takes his vessel about quite a bit.'

'Across the Channel?'

'Who knows where they go, but quite often enough for pleasure.'

'They?'

'With his wife as crew. She's a good sailor.'

'Pretty?'

Jenkins gave a short laugh. 'I wouldn't say pretty, exactly. Weather-beaten, more like. Wears the trousers, too.'

Detective Inspector Sloan's thoughts went soaring off on another tack. 'Accountants do themselves pretty well then . . .'

'They say she's the one with the money.'

Detective Inspector Sloan made a note. Marrying money was exactly the sort of legend that money-launderers wanted to accrue around those who had much more of this world's goods than could be accounted for by their usual circumstances.

He amplified this fact afterwards for the benefit of Detective Constable Crosby. 'There's plenty of ways of explaining sudden wealth away,' he said to that conscionable young officer, who never had any money whatsoever to spare at the end of the month. 'A big win on the lottery is the most popular.'

'Could happen to anyone,' agreed Crosby wryly.

'Premium Bonds.' Sloan knew them all by now. 'A bit of good fortune on the pools . . .'

'Rich relations?' put in Crosby, showing interest in the theory.

'Sometimes, but most people know that great expectations can be a snare and a delusion.' This reminded him to tell Crosby to locate one Peter Caversham in Luston.

'Will do,' promised Crosby, brightening. The road between Berebury and Luston was the best in the county.

'And last wills and testaments can be checked a bit too easily with the probate office for your really experienced money-launderer,' warned Sloan, returning to his theme. 'But a lot of people are fooled by someone with a reputation for having a sharp eye for the stock market.' Any spare funds in the Sloan household economy went straight into the building society against a rainy day. At the moment they didn't amount to enough to withstand the lightest of showers.

'You can be lucky with horses,' suggested Crosby.

'So they say,' agreed Sloan, who knew how rare a commodity a really good eye for horseflesh was. 'Don't forget bookies know who has big money, and they don't easily forget who's won it off them . . .'

'But, sir,' said Detective Constable Crosby incontrovertibly, 'that Derek whose wake we went to last night had got loadsamoney some other way still.'

*

Behind the scenes the Greatorex Museum presented a very different picture on committee days. Today was that of the monthly meeting of the Museums and Amenities Committee of Berebury Council, and Howard Air was in the chair, flanked by his chief officer, Marcus Fixby-Smith. Hilary Collins, the latter's deputy, was therefore holding the fort in the outside world, and it was she who took the message that the mummy had been found in Whimbrel House.

'Undamaged, I hope?' asked Fixby-Smith anxiously as the two men came quickly out of the Committee Room. 'No one's touched it, have they, Hilary?'

'It had been stood on end, that's all,' Hilary Collins assured him.

'That's all!' exploded the museum curator. 'Why, that could have done untold damage. Don't the police know better than that?'

'Steady on, Marcus,' said Howard Air, still a little out of breath from hurrying back to the curator's room. 'Remember, it might not have been the police who stood it on end in the first place.'

'It might have been the same person who killed that poor girl.' Hilary Collins was sufficiently plain, capable and conscientious to feel free to speak her mind.

'It almost certainly was,' pointed out Howard Air realistically.

Marcus Fixby-Smith collapsed like a pricked balloon. 'I hadn't thought of that . . .' His voice trailed away into silence.

'You can't afford not to face facts in my business,' said Air. He had the lined features of a man who looked

114

as if he had not so much faced facts in life as met them head-on. 'And nor can you in yours, Marcus. This means more trouble.'

In contrast with the stocky businessman, Marcus Fixby-Smith looked a bundle of nervous affectations. He had been struck by yet another unattractive thought. 'You do realize, both of you, that from now until the end of time, whatever we do, the public will be coming to see Rodoheptah for the wrong reasons.'

In a voice totally devoid of inflection, Hilary Collins said, 'Just think, Marcus, what that will do to our visitor numbers.'

As always, unsure which way to take what she said, he ignored it. 'What I can't understand is why the body and the mummy were switched.'

'I can't help you there,' said Howard Air, scrubbing his brow in thought. 'But there will have been a reason. You can bet your bottom dollar on that.'

'And,' wailed Fixby-Smith, 'what on earth are we going to do about the press now? They'll have a field day when they hear about Rodoheptah turning up in a broom cupboard.'

'Oh, it was in a broom cupboard, was it?' remarked Howard Air. 'I didn't hear you say that bit, Hilary.'

'I didn't say it,' she murmured quietly, her eyes on Marcus Fixby-Smith.

'It must have been in the broom cupboard,' protested the museum curator. 'It stands to reason. There wasn't anywhere else near enough in the house to hide something like that.'

Marcus Fixby-Smith might not have known what

Hilary Collins had been thinking the minute before. He had no doubts at all now what was in her mind at this minute.

Or in Howard Air's.

Chapter Ten

Creased

'I trust Squeak is still doing well, Inspector?' Alison Kirk waved the two policemen into the kitchen at the Calleshire Animal Sanctuary ahead of her, shaking a finger at an Airedale and a West Highland terrier both of which were barking at the policemen. 'Down, Rover, down, Rags . . . these are friends.'

'Squeak's fine,' said Sloan warmly, 'except that he scratched Crosby here the last time he was at the house.'

'Some cats don't like the attention that visitors get,' she said seriously.

'And the scar hasn't quite healed yet.' Detective Constable Crosby extended his wounded left wrist for her inspection. 'Look, you can still see where he did it.'

'Jealous,' contributed Jennifer, the younger of the Kirk sisters. 'They like being top cat in the household.'

Alison Kirk indicated two spare chairs and sat herself down at the kitchen table. 'Now, Inspector, don't tell me that you came over here just to talk about a black tom-cat with a white waistcoat and four white paws.'

'No,' said Sloan. 'We came to talk to you about your late nephew.'

'Derek?'

'Derek,' agreed Sloan. 'Or, more precisely, about the rather large sum of money of which he would seem to have become possessed not long before he died.'

'Very large sum,' Alison corrected him unexpectedly. 'It absolutely amazed us.' She turned to her sister. 'Didn't it, Jennifer?'

'We didn't think it was safe for him to have all that money in cash in his house.'

'Quite dangerous, really,' said Alison.

'But he said he hadn't anything to lose.'

'You see,' said Sloan, choosing his words with care, 'it might help us over some other inquiries to know exactly where all that money came from.'

'He didn't say,' said the elder woman.

'Come, Miss Kirk . . .'

'Come nothing,' she retorted spiritedly. 'He told us that the money was really and truly his to do what he liked with; a proper windfall.'

'I see.' Detective Inspector Sloan took this with the customary police pinch of salt. Even windfalls could – and sometimes did – carry a touch of skulduggery about them. Windfalls had entered the language from the medieval laws – the forest laws.

'And only his,' put in Jennifer Kirk, reaching for the milk jug. 'No one else's.'

'And, moreover, he insisted he was going to do exactly what he liked with it, too, whatever anyone else said,' carried on Alison.

'Quite so,' said Sloan. Real windfalls were trees which had fallen upon the King's highway and which the peas-

antry were then entitled to collect and burn for fuel –
a canny self-financing medieval method of keeping the
roadway clear. The skulduggery came in when the ver-
derer – the judicial officer of the King's forest – found
the roots of a tree half chopped away in the right direction to encourage it to fall on the highway.

'Down to the very last penny before he died,' said
Derek's aunt. 'Which, poor boy, he knew wouldn't be
long.'

'Doctors are franker than they used to be,' put in
Jennifer Kirk. 'Not so mealy-mouthed.'

'Difficult to live happily knowing you're going to die
soon,' agreed Sloan.

'You can say that again,' murmured Jennifer. 'It
didn't help him. Us, perhaps, but not him.'

'If you're young, that is,' Sloan added by way of
amendment. He'd never forgotten that poor old man in
one of Geoffrey Chaucer's *Canterbury Tales* who had
been wandering about seeking Death everywhere but
never finding him. There were more people like that
these days, too, than there used to be, modern medicine
being what it had become.

'That's where animals do better than we do,
Inspector,' observed Jennifer Kirk. 'They may live in
fear of the here and now, but not of the hereafter like
Derek did.'

Alison Kirk sniffed. 'We all know Derek wasn't
perfect and Aids is a terrible disease; but he wasn't
either a thief or a liar and if he told us that money was
his to give away then it was.'

Jennifer Kirk nodded vigorously. 'He said he was

determined to use up as much of his money as he could while he could.'

Alison Kirk raised her hand to her face to brush away a tear and said, 'He didn't quite manage to use it all up, though, Inspector.'

'He died first,' explained Jennifer Kirk.

'But he had a good try at spending the lot,' said her sister. 'A very good try.'

'That's what we had heard,' said Sloan.

Alison Kirk looked round the untidy, old-fashioned kitchen. 'He gave us quite a bit for our animals here. We're going to spend some of it on a set of new dog kennels.' She turned to the two dogs. 'Did you hear that, my darlings?'

Jennifer said, 'We've had a legacy, too . . .' She pushed a couple of cats off the table and belatedly covered the milk jug. 'It never rains but it pours.'

'From an old soldier in Berebury called Caversham.' Alison got to her feet as a kettle came to the boil on the top of an iron stove. 'Very welcome, I must say.'

'We'd also heard about that,' said Sloan truthfully, deciding not to mention the rather different inheritance that the police had had from the same old soldier in Berebury.

'Which we're going to spend on fencing the paddock for the horses,' said Jennifer.

'And Dunce,' said Alison.

'Dunce?' asked Crosby.

'The donkey.'

Jennifer Kirk gave both men a surprisingly sweet

smile. 'That'll please your Inspector Harpe after the shenanigans the other night, won't it?'

Alison plonked a sturdy teapot down on the wooden table and set four mugs beside it. 'Now, then, Inspector, are you going to tell us what all this is about or not?'

One of the characteristics which policemen have in common with members of the medical profession is that they customarily respond to questions with another question; not an answer. Detective Inspector Sloan was no exception to this rule. 'When Derek spoke about this money, how did he himself refer to it – apart from as a windfall, that is?'

'As his own, his very own,' said Alison Kirk, pouring the tea.

'He gave us some money for the Lake Ryrie Project in Lasserta, as well,' chimed in Jennifer. 'They're going to enclose some of the land there to protect some very rare monkeys and call it after Derek. He would have liked that.'

'He knew how strongly we felt about the Lake Ryrie Reserve, too,' Alison said earnestly. 'It's no good our just caring for the species in this country, you know. That would be selfish.'

'The welfare of animals everywhere should be everyone's concern,' said Jennifer Kirk sternly, 'but especially of endangered species such as those monkeys there.'

'I'm afraid Lasserta doesn't have a very good track record of kindness to animals,' said her sister.

'So how do you go about supporting the Lake Ryrie Project in the ordinary way?' asked Sloan.

'In the ordinary way?' echoed Alison, pushing a bowl towards them. 'Help yourselves to sugar.'

'Without Derek.'

'Just like we raise funds for our animal sanctuary here.' The elder Miss Kirk waved an arm to encompass the range of sundry kennels, cattery, stables and out-buildings which comprised the outfit. 'It's the usual: sales of work, coffee mornings, flag days . . .'

Detective Inspector Sloan, conscientious police officer that he was, made a note to check on the funding of both the Calleshire Animal Sanctuary and the Lake Ryrie Project in Lasserta. Money-launderers could work in some very strange places – the stranger, the better, from their point of view. And if it involved a change of country and currency, so much the better. The audit trail, enemy of the drug dealer and friend of the fiscal authorities, didn't cross national borders very well: it regularly lost its way at the point where jurisdictions transferred from one sovereign state to another, and drug dealers knew it. And it often proved quite difficult to pick up again on the other side of the sea. Like Tam O'Shanter pursued, safety lay in crossing the water.

Sloan brought his mind back to the matter in hand with a jerk and asked the two women if they knew a girl called Jill Carter.

They shook their heads in unison while Alison Kirk turned to Detective Constable Crosby and said, 'You wouldn't like a kitten, too, would you, Constable? We've got plenty more where Squeak came from and two queens in kindle . . .'

*

Detective Constable Crosby looked up as Sloan came in. 'Mrs Sloan rang, sir, but she said it wasn't urgent.'

'Right.' It wasn't like Margaret to telephone him at the police station in the middle of the day. Later on, perhaps, if he was worryingly late in coming off duty, but not otherwise. 'I'll ring her when I'm free.'

'She sounded a bit cross,' volunteered Crosby.

Detective Inspector Sloan, no fool, picked up the telephone at once. The chill factor was immediately apparent when he got through to his home number. 'A problem?' he asked uneasily.

'There's been something arrive for you,' his wife said distantly.

'For me?' He ran his mind swiftly over his personal purchases for the last couple of weeks but nothing in his memory surfaced.

'By carrier.'

He was more puzzled still.

'It's marked "Next Day Delivery".'

'But . . .'

'And "Open Immediately".'

'But does it say who it's from?'

'Lingard and Lingard.'

'The rose people?'

A mild snort travelled down the line. 'How did you guess?'

'Roses?'

'What else?' she enquired ironically.

'I didn't order any roses.'

'I thought,' she said elliptically, 'that we'd already agreed about that.'

'We had.'

'It looks,' she said coldly, 'very like the special collection of patio standards that we decided we couldn't afford.'

'We did decide.' Sloan hadn't had the slightest difficulty in hearing the stress on the word 'we' twice in that sentence.

'And we still can't afford them,' she said pointedly.

'No.'

'So . . .'

'So I don't know anything about them.'

'They're marked "Urgent and Perishable" too . . .'

'So they may be,' said Sloan, pulling his notebook nearer.

'Do I put them in water then?' she asked acidly.

'You don't put them anywhere,' ordered Margaret's husband, thinking fast and suddenly galvanized into action. 'You leave them strictly alone!'

'But . . .' she protested.

'Don't touch them!' He was almost shouting now.

'All right. If you say so.'

'Keep away from them, understand? As far away as you can. Do nothing at all until I get there.' He slammed the phone down. 'Come on, Crosby. Don't just stand there! Let's get moving, and fast!'

Chapter Eleven

Torn

There was only one room in the overcrowded offices of Pearson, Worrow and Gisby, Chartered Accountants, which was sacrosanct to the persons of Nigel Worrow and Jim Pearson and in which they were never to be interrupted. Kenneth Gisby was deemed still too young to be privy to it. Although it rejoiced in the name of the Partners' Room, it was rarely used as such, being both small and inconvenient. It did, however, have a locked cupboard to which only the two men enjoyed the keys.

Inside the cupboard was a bottle of very good single malt whisky. This was usually opened to mark the minor ups and downs in the usually humdrum world of auditing other people's figures.

Today was not humdrum, but Worrow waved away Pearson's sketched offer of a dram without hesitation. 'No, thanks, Jim. Not now. I need to think.'

'We both do,' said Pearson. He sank into the chair opposite and added significantly, 'And about rather a lot of things.'

'Starting with poor Jill . . .' said his partner, still visibly shaken by the news.

'It's almost always the boyfriend, remember,' said

Pearson, in an unconscious echo of the opinion of Superintendent Leeyes.

'Then we don't have anything to worry about,' concluded Worrow, nevertheless looking a very worried man.

Pearson shook his head. 'I'm not so sure about that, Nigel. I think we do.'

'What do you mean?' Nigel Worrow looked searchingly at his partner. 'I would have thought that it's only if it wasn't the boyfriend that we needed to worry. Anyway it'll take the police quite a time to be sure that it's him. Thornhill was the name, wasn't it?'

'Colin,' said Pearson, who was the one who was keenest on using Christian names.

'And,' said Nigel Worrow, 'while they're making sure it's – er – Colin, you can bet your bottom dollar they'll sift through everything else here they can lay their hands on.'

'Perhaps,' said Pearson, 'I'll have a whisky myself anyway.'

'You do realize, don't you, that the police can probably go on a fishing expedition here now even without a court order . . .'

'I suppose anything's possible in the sacred name of justice,' agreed Pearson gloomily.

'And there might be some small matters that take a bit of explaining . . .'

'Every firm in existence must have some files they wouldn't want the police asking questions about.' Jim Pearson took a sip of his whisky. 'Especially in our line of business.'

'It's our line of business that I have in mind,' said Nigel Worrow.

'And would you happen to have anything particular in mind?' enquired Jim Pearson delicately.

'There's a client to whom I gave a good deal of advice about the possibilities of a viatical settlement not long ago,' said Worrow.

'So? Granted, viatical settlements don't crop up all that often,' said Pearson. 'And we aren't all experts. I haven't had one in ages.'

'It's not everyone,' agreed Worrow, 'who's been told they're going to die long before they can get their hands on the proceeds of an endowment insurance policy that's a good deal more healthy than they are.'

'True. It's when the medicos say it'll be within two years, isn't it?'

'They're not so fussy about the predicted time of death as they used to be,' said Worrow. 'Anyway, I gave this man – he was the nephew of those two Kirk sisters who have been clients of ours for years – my advice. I said he ought to go to one of the viatical settlement companies who would take a second medical opinion and then consider buying his endowment policy on the strength of it or, of course, alternatively, he could just put the policy up for auction and get what he could for it.'

'You do have to spell out all the options these days,' nodded Pearson sagely. 'So what's wrong with his cutting and running like that? I'd have given the man exactly the same advice if he'd consulted me.'

'He didn't do either of those two things,' said Worrow sombrely.

'So what's the problem, Nigel? Clients don't have to do everything we tell 'em to.' He essayed a grin. 'They only have to pay us for advising them on their best course of action.'

His partner did not return his smile. 'The problem is that he still raised a hell of a lot of money on it somehow, and then went and died.'

Jim Pearson took considerably more than a sip of his whisky. 'I see what you mean,' he said slowly. 'And you're saying that we should have told the proper authorities that it must have been a suspicious transaction, even though we've no idea who was party to it.'

'I think that's the theory, Jim; although you know as well as I do that the legislation on this sort of thing is changing all the time.'

'And now we don't know where your client got the money.'

'Not a clue,' said Nigel Worrow. He braced himself. 'All I know is that he died early yesterday morning.'

'Sir,' began Sloan stiltedly, 'I have to report an attempt at bribery.'

Superintendent Leeyes grunted. 'It wasn't a bomb, then.'

'A dozen rose bushes were delivered to my home address . . .' As far as Sloan was concerned the rose bushes had come with the same intention as high explosive.

'Rose bushes?' The superintendent's bushy eyebrows almost disappeared up his forehead. 'You're not trying to wind me up about all this, I hope, Sloan, because if so . . .'

'Special ones for the patio: a particular collection, very expensive, that I had wanted especially, but I – we – decided we couldn't afford.'

Superintendent Leeyes grunted again.

'Dispatched sir, by carrier last night from Nottinghamshire to my home address, by the firm I usually deal with.'

'Sloan, are you quite sure that these roses weren't a surprise present from your wife?'

'Absolutely sure, sir,' he said stiffly. 'I can assure you that possibility doesn't arise. Apart from anything else, sir, Margaret doesn't particularly care for rose bushes.'

'But the order should be able to be traced easily enough,' commented Leeyes. 'The firm . . .'

'The special collection was paid for in cash yesterday,' said Sloan, who had just done some urgent telephoning to Lingard and Lingard. 'By a London courier. For immediate dispatch.'

'Expense no object, then,' commented Leeyes.

'Exactly, sir.'

'The courier?'

'The rose people didn't notice anything particular about him. All they can say is that he was dressed up to the eyebrows in black motorcycle leathers and didn't take his helmet off.'

'Any message with the roses?'

' "A foretaste of summer", written on the card at the

dictation of the courier,' said Sloan. He himself didn't have any particular difficulty in interpreting this as: plenty more of everything from where these came from.

Neither did Superintendent Leeyes.

'I have started, of course, sir, to go into the question of exactly who knew that these particular roses were just what I wanted, but had already decided I – we – couldn't afford.' This was a sore point. In his opinion secrets of the family purse should be kept as private as those of the bedroom and they hadn't been.

What had emerged – until, that is, his wife had heatedly declined to be cross-questioned like a common police suspect another single minute – was the fact that Margaret had just happened to mention the patio collection of rose bushes to a very pleasant woman who had just happened to have been sitting next to her at her ladies afternoon meeting the day before.

No, she hadn't known her.

No, she had never seen her before.

No, she didn't know her name. She had simply assumed she was a new member.

No, Margaret had not brought the subject of patio roses up. They had begun by talking about winning the lottery and what they would do with the money if they did.

There was no harm in dreaming. Everyone was allowed to dream.

Yes, from there they had gone on to discussing more affordable pleasures. That was what everybody always did. Didn't he know that?

Oh, she'd forgotten. Policemen only ever asked questions. They didn't answer them.

Third degree, more like.

No, she hadn't forgotten that was American.

Oh, all right then, if it was so important.

Then this woman had said that she didn't mind about not winning the lottery but what she really wanted was a new garden gate.

Yes, naturally then Margaret had mentioned the rose bush collection and if there had been anything wrong in doing that she would very much like to know what it was because she hadn't signed the Official Secrets Act even if he had . . .

'I must say they're pretty quick workers, sir.'

'They've had a week, haven't they? If this girl, Jill Carter, was killed last Friday.'

'Sorry, sir, I was forgetting.'

Superintendent Leeyes tapped his pen on his desk. 'It just goes to show, Sloan, what you can do with unlimited resources.'

'Sir?'

'It's all very well for some people . . .'

'My wife?' said Sloan, puzzled.

'Drug barons,' said Leeyes succinctly. 'They've got all the money in the world.'

That was what Jenny, the forensic accountant, had said, too.

'And all the time, too,' said Sloan, conscious of how much there was still to be done.

'And we haven't either the time or the money,' commented Leeyes. He sniffed. 'Especially not the money.'

'No, sir,' Sloan hastened to agree. Other police forces had Drug Squads; Berebury had Sloan and Crosby. 'These roses, sir . . .'

'Ah, yes, Sloan. The roses.' He leaned back in his chair. 'What do you propose doing about them?'

Detective Inspector Sloan took a deep breath. 'As I see it, sir, we have two options.'

'Go on.'

'I can send them back to Lingard and Lingard and get an eye kept there . . . Or,' said Sloan, 'I could put them out on my patio and see what happens.'

'Any further developments might well be interesting,' conceded the superintendent. 'Very interesting. Be sure to keep me in the picture.'

'Here's your week's money, Goddard, and my brother says you needn't come Monday.'

Sid Wetherspoon's brother had his uses; especially when he wasn't present. On some occasions when Fred Wetherspoon wasn't there, Sid would begin his spiel with 'My brother and I'; especially if he didn't relish what he had to say.

This was one of those occasions. Sid went on, 'My brother and I, young feller, don't think that you're cut out for working in the removals business. Not really.'

'No, Mr Wetherspoon.' Wayne Goddard didn't bother to raise his eyebrows. There was nothing at which he needed even to feign surprise. He had realized most of the week that his days with Wetherspoon and Wetherspoon were numbered. The manager of the Job Centre wouldn't like it of course, but then he never did; and anyway he ought to be used to Wayne's being stood off at the end of his first week with each new employer by now. On the whole, he would probably be more upset than Wayne himself was.

'You see,' Wetherspooon said, not unkindly, 'you haven't got the muscle . . .'

Actually, now he came to think about it, Sid had never seen Wayne Goddard's muscles, since – no matter how hot it was – the lad hadn't once rolled his sleeves up to get down to work. It was one of Sid's grievances, only these days employers weren't allowed to have grievances. Only workers seemed to be entitled to those now.

'No,' agreed the puny Wayne without rancour.

'So we – my brother and I – think you'd do better in some other sort of work.' Sid was making a real effort to choose his words carefully. These days it was more difficult, too, to sack people than it had been. To say nothing of then not being able to take on who you wanted instead. It was the lurking fear of having to employ a woman under the new equal opportunity legislation that had very nearly led to Wayne's keeping his job with Wetherspoon and Wetherspoon, as the lesser of two evils.

'Yes, Mr Wetherspoon.'

'Mind you, boy, it hasn't got anything to do with those two policemen coming round here wanting to know everything we've done this week at Whimbrel House.'

'No?' Wayne Goddard's eyebrows did go up at this.

'No,' said Sid untruthfully. Actually, it had been the last straw as far as the brothers Wetherspoon were concerned. It wasn't that Sid had minded being grilled by Detective Inspector Sloan; he had been quite happy at his own answers. It was the uneasiness that Sid had felt at Wayne Goddard's responses which had stayed with him after the police had left, and it was still worrying him.

'Right then. I'll be on my way.' Goddard reached out a hand for his pay packet.

Sid kept his hand on the envelope. 'All the forms you need are in there...'

'Right,' said Goddard again, hand still extended.

'... but there's something I'd like to know before you go.'

'What's that then?'

'Who did you tell that we'd looked round Whimbrel House on Tuesday first while we sized the job up for yesterday?'

'Me?' Goddard's face assumed its innocent choirboy expression. 'No one. No one at all. Honest, Mr Wetherspoon.'

'You must remember, gentlemen,' said Dr Dabbe, emphasizing his point by waving an alarming-looking instrument of unknown purpose at the two detectives across his desk at the mortuary, 'that, in the words of a very distinguished epidemiologist, "Death certificates are merely passports to civilized burial".'

'And to keep the coroner happy,' said Sloan sardonically.

Dabbe smiled. 'I understand this mummy isn't going to get a civilized burial.'

'It's going to the Greatorex Museum,' said Detective Constable Crosby.

'There you are, then,' said the pathologist, putting the instrument down, and picking up a pen instead.

'But only,' said Detective Inspector Sloan pointedly, 'when Mr Locombe-Stableford is completely satisfied that it is of purely archaeological interest.'

'Which, as I explained to you yesterday in similar circumstances, a radiological examination should confirm.'

'Today,' murmured Detective Constable Crosby under his breath, 'if not yesterday.'

'That,' the pathologist shot a wry glance in the inspector's direction, 'is the theory, anyway. However, I have arranged for a very well-known palaeopathologist, known to Marcus Fixby-Smith, to assist me in my examination of the mummy. He's on his way.'

Crosby grinned. 'That should keep both the coroner and the curator happy.'

'Doctor,' intervened Sloan hastily, 'yesterday you mentioned the dangers of opening up the actual mummy . . .' Had it really only been yesterday? It seemed days ago. 'Now that we've actually got a mummy, I'd like to know what those dangers are.' Having life insurance was all very well but it didn't compare with having life.

'Anthrax is the main risk,' said Dr Dabbe, at once

becoming hortative. '*Bacillus anthracis* forms spores and these do exist for very long periods in a viable stage outside the human body.' He twirled his pen between his fingers. 'Didn't you know? That's what makes it into a weapon of war. Relatively inexpensive, too.'

'War?' echoed Crosby, who was sure he'd already been taught everything about man's inhumanity to man at the Police Training College.

'Very popular with some of our enemies, anthrax,' the doctor informed him. 'They stocked it, you know, even if it didn't get used.'

'Not us, though?' said Crosby.

'Oh, we stocked it, too,' said Dr Dabbe airily, 'purely for the purposes of scientific research, of course. On an island in Gruinard Bay in Scotland. They say it's all right now.'

All Detective Inspector Sloan could think of was that character in the radio programme ITMA who had been sick but said she 'was all right now'. He hoped the same could be said for Gruinard Island.

'But in a mummy?' persisted Crosby, still anxious.

'Oh, yes, my boy. The spores have been found in ancient mummies before now, as I shall explain to the coroner if the X-rays are inconclusive.'

'I thought anthrax was a disease of sheep,' murmured Sloan without thinking. He, like most policemen, had in his time pinned up many a public notice about warble fly.

'Well, it is one of the zoonoses, Sloan,' expounded the pathologist happily, 'and the clostridia are species specific.'

'Does that mean what I think it means?' asked Sloan.

Dr Dabbe beamed. 'It does. One variety is actually called Woolsorter's Disease.'

'Well, I never,' said Crosby.

'That's the pulmonary variety,' said the pathologist.

One of the few judicial remarks that Sloan remembered was 'Let us to our muttons'. He didn't quote it now. He thought it was about time they got away from sheep. Instead he said firmly, 'The mummy can only go to the museum, of course, when the police too are completely satisfied that the mummy itself has no essential connection with the body of the girl who was in the *cartonnage.*'

Dr Dabbe looked over the other instruments on the tray before selecting a long probe. 'Shall we say that the *cartonnage* was probably, as Shakespeare put it so well, only "A shell of death"?'

'We think that Jill Carter was dead when she was put in it,' Sloan informed him, taking this literally. 'The forensic people have confirmed that from their examination of the wood. They think she'd stopped bleeding by the time she was put in there.'

Dabbe nodded. 'That blow on the head would have killed her outright. By the way, I don't know if it's important to you chaps or not but she wasn't pregnant.' He waved a hand in the direction of his office. 'It'll all be in my report.'

'Was she on drugs, doctor?' asked Sloan.

'Not in my opinion. At least, I could find no immediate evidence of banned substances and I can assure you that there were no macroscopic signs of drug taking: ropy veins, injection sites, infected haematomata and so forth.'

'Thank you,' said Sloan, making a note.

'But I can't tell you definitely yet whether she had liver damage as a consequence of suffering from one or more of the happy family of hepatitises.' He paused. 'Or should that be hepatiti?'

'I couldn't say, I'm sure, doctor,' said Sloan repressively. If there was one change in police procedure which had really made him wonder at the modern world, it was the official turning of the police blind eye to the needle exchange system set up in Berebury by the over-socially-conscious to save drug addicts from the blood diseases spread by sharing needles for their self-injection of proscribed substances. Nelson himself couldn't have done it better. Cost-effective in the broadest sense was how the idea had been sold to an outraged but outwardly compliant Calleshire Constabulary.

'But all will be revealed,' said the pathologist sedately, 'when I get the lab reports on the deceased back.'

'In due course,' said Crosby, totally without inflection.

'What we're really interested in now, doctor,' intervened Sloan hastily, 'is the timing of events.'

'Where and when,' Crosby supplemented this quite unnecessarily.

The pathologist looked suddenly serious again. 'In my opinion, gentlemen, Jill Carter had been dead roughly about a week before I examined her.'

'Like the day she went missing?' suggested Crosby. 'Last Friday.'

'Possibly. Going first on the expected post-mortem lividity and then on the later changes in that – alteration at the points where there would have been pressure from a wooden casing designed for someone else and so forth – I should say she had been dead for some days before she was encased in the *cartonnage* in which I first saw her, and had been in it for at least twenty-four hours.'

Detective Inspector Sloan had been thinking as well as listening. 'That means she was parked somewhere else before she was put in there.'

Dr Dabbe agreed. 'But perhaps that is more likely to be definitely established from other than medical evidence.'

'They're still going over her clothing at forensic,' said Crosby, 'and going all over the house, too.'

'And we've got a team going over the car park where the girl was last seen,' said Sloan. 'There may be blood there . . .'

He did not feel it necessary to add that the same skilled team of specialists in forensic evidence were about to examine the interior of the car belonging to one of her employers – the accountant and amateur yachtsman Nigel Worrow.

Chapter Twelve

Worn

'Anthony Heber-Hibbs here . . .'

'This is Detective Inspector Sloan of the Calleshire Constabulary, your excellency, and I'm ringing from England.' Had he got that right, Sloan wondered. He wasn't used to addressing ambassadors, even if it was over the telephone; and halfway round the world to boot.

'How may I help you, Inspector?' said a pleasant-sounding very English voice.

'Just a routine inquiry, sir, about an animal protection reserve in Lasserta.' Offhand, Sloan couldn't even remember what the postage stamps of Lasserta looked like – and he'd learned geography by philately.

'The Lake Ryrie Project? What about it?'

'This may sound a little silly to you, sir, but we're ringing to confirm that the reserve actually exists.'

'I'll say. Does a good job here, too. Tell me more.'

'That's all we really needed to know,' said Sloan apologetically, 'but we are involved in a money-laundering inquiry here.'

'In lemps, Inspector?' His excellency sounded amused. 'Are you sure it's in lemps?'

'Lemps?'

'That's the currency here.'

'No, no, sir. It's just that we know one of the more popular ways of getting illicit funds out of any country is to invent a plausible but totally imaginary set-up somewhere abroad, and send the money there under that pretext.'

Anthony Heber-Hibbs said alertly, 'I get you, Inspector.'

'Preferably,' added Sloan, 'where the imaginary project can reasonably be supposed to have funding from other countries, too.'

'Like the Lake Ryrie Project . . .'

'Exactly.'

'So that anyone enquiring could be told the money is coming from somewhere else,' mused the ambassador thoughtfully.

'Preferably from somewhere where the enquirer doesn't have any jurisdiction,' said Sloan tightly. This was a perennial sore point with those who sought to arraign lawbreakers and had to watch them slip through their fingers as a consequence of diplomatic niceties, corrupt regimes, ancient treaties and the fallout from old wars.

'Well, Inspector,' observed Heber-Hibbs, 'while I can't actually hear the animals howling from the embassy, I can assure you that they are in the Lake Ryrie compound all right.'

'Thank you, sir.' Sloan made a note. 'That means there is one avenue of inquiry that we here needn't pursue any further – which will be a help.'

'Especially the last few Piddock's Jasper,' Mr Heber-Hibbs informed him.

'Pardon, sir?'

'The Kingdom of Lasserta is the only place in the world where Piddock's Jasper still exists. A protected species, of course.'

'Ah, I understand, sir. A rare breed.'

'A charming little jungle monkey, which as you may imagine, has to be kept at a considerable distance from the lions. They keep hoping they will breed in captivity here – the Jaspers, not the lions.'

'Yes, sir, I'm sure. Well, that's all I need to know.' He stopped, struck by a sudden thought. 'Do you grow opium in Lasserta?'

'Bless you, no, Inspector.' The ambassador laughed. 'I'm happy to say that pineapples are our main export crop. As far as I know they are as pure as driven snow. No, perhaps snow isn't the right analogy if your money-laundering has anything to do with drug dealing.'

'No, sir. I mean, yes.' Detective Inspector Sloan was ready to dismiss pineapples – until he remembered cloves. There had once been a famous attempt to corner the market in cloves and hold the commercial world to ransom. There was no world shortage of pineapples, though, that he knew about. 'Is anything else grown much in Lasserta?'

'Oh, yes. Bananas, short and curly but very good, mangoes, and a rather special sweet variety of a Lassertan rhubarb. That sells very well.'

Just in time, Detective Inspector Sloan suppressed

an unfortunate reference to a banana republic. Lasserta was, after all, a kingdom.

'Our commercial attaché would be able to fill you in properly on the trading here, Inspector,' Heber-Hibbs was saying. 'He'd be your man for that sort of detail, if it's important.'

'No thank you, sir,' said Sloan. 'But it's good to hear about a flourishing economy overseas rather than a corrupt one.'

There was a significant pause and then the ambassador said gently, as one instructing the young and innocent, 'There are some foreign countries, Inspector, where it is accepted that a little corruption is good for trade.'

'Really, sir?' he said coolly.

'But rest assured that the exports from here which find their way to your Calleshire are the pick of the crop.'

'Howard Air Limited?' divined Sloan without too much difficulty.

'One of the biggest customers for our pineapples and the subsidiary crops, too,' Heber-Hibbs said. 'And very particular about quality.'

Detective Inspector Sloan said he was glad to hear it.

'He's the moving spirit behind the Lake Ryrie Project, by the way. Ask him. He'll tell you all about it.'

'Well, not exactly progress, sir,' said Detective Constable Crosby cautiously when he answered Sloan's summons to his office. 'More like getting some routine information in.'

'Such as?'

'The fingerprint people can't find anything useful on the *cartonnage*,' said Crosby.

'I wouldn't have supposed that they would,' said Sloan irritably. 'We're not dealing with amateurs.'

'And the Scenes of Crime outfit confirm that there are no exterior signs of breaking and entering at Whimbrel House. So whoever's been coming and going's had a key.'

'Coming and going?' barked Sloan sharply.

'Yes, sir. Forensic say that what they did find at Whimbrel House . . .' He turned over the page of his notebook with provocative deliberation.

'Well?' snapped Sloan. He wasn't going to play games with Crosby, but sorting him out would have to wait a little longer.

' . . . were traces of heroin in the kitchen,' finished Crosby with *empressement*.

'They did, did they?' said Sloan, thinking quickly.

'Especially on the table.'

'A thieves' kitchen.'

'Puts a different complexion on things, doesn't it, sir?'

'I think, Crosby,' said Sloan, applying an even older analogy, 'we may even have identified a modern den of iniquity.'

'Yes, sir.'

'Though we mustn't forget that both Sid Wetherspoon and Wayne Goddard say that nobody had their key between Tuesday when they first went round there, and Thursday when they arrived with their removal van,' said Sloan. The visit from the removal men must have had some consequences for whoever was using Whimbrel House for nefarious purposes. He would have to work on that later.

'If you can believe Wayne Goddard, sir, then you can believe anything.'

Detective Inspector Sloan reminded his subordinate that it was every police officer's job not to believe anything, ever, until he or she had hard evidence to prove whatever it was.

'Yes, sir. They say the key hung on a hook just inside Sid's office,' pressed on Crosby, undeterred by this little homily, 'with a number of other keys being held for the same reasons.'

'Labelled, I dare say,' said Sloan bitterly, 'just to make things easier for anyone who took it. If they did.' What had made things more straightforward for the police was this link between the death of Jill Carter and the drugs scene. It was something much more positive than that one of her employers had a yacht at Kinnisport and went on long sea trips in the Channel.

'Not exactly labelled, sir,' said Crosby. 'It was on one of Puckle's usual keyrings. The firm have their own.'

'I call that advertising,' said Sloan. 'Now, how have you got on with your forensic genealogy?'

Crosby looked blank.

'The heirs of Colonel Caversham.'

'Oh.' His face cleared. He reached for his notebook. 'The colonel's brother was killed at Dunkirk. His name is on the Staple St James war memorial. He only had one son who was called Gerald . . .'

'He who ran off with somebody's daughter?'

Crosby nodded. 'She was called Sybil.'

'And they were married.' Sloan was fairly confident about this. The bend sinister would have put any children of this union quite out of the running for the Caversham family money and thus have been of no interest to Messrs Puckle, Puckle and Nunnery, executors and trustees.

'Yes, sir. The marriage took place in a register office in London. Mr Puckle had got as far as finding that out.'

'And then?'

'And then the trail goes a bit cold,' said Crosby. 'The colonel simply told the solicitors that his nephew had gone abroad.'

'And?'

'And what, sir?'

'And did they have any sons?'

'That's what no one can find out for sure, sir. All we can establish from all the proper authorities is that someone called Gerald Caversham died, aged seventy-five, last year in India.'

'Big country, India,' observed Sloan.

'The solicitors have had agents make inquiries out there but they can't come up with anything positive about the couple having had – er – male issue.'

'Getting nowhere fast, in fact,' said Sloan.

'And that is all that anyone can discover at this stage, sir,' said Crosby. 'Us, too.'

Detective Inspector Sloan slowly digested the implications of this. 'I can see Puckle's problem as executor over the inheritance of the settled estate.' It was beginning to look as if Jarndyce versus Jarndyce might have nothing on the Executors and Trustees of Caversham deceased versus Caversham living; although the connection, if any, with the use of Whimbrel House for the distribution, storage or usage of heroin eluded him. 'Not easy.'

'It could be proved that Gerald and Sybil Caversham had had sons, sir; if they had them, that is,' Crosby put it awkwardly. 'But not that they hadn't had any, if they hadn't; if you know what I mean.'

'I think I do,' said Sloan gravely. The constable had made the not irrelevant statement 'Yes, we have no bananas' sound positively simple and straightforward. 'And, if they hadn't, and it could be proved that they hadn't, then, failing all others, a man called Peter Caversham scoops the pool.'

'He lives at Water Lane, Luston, sir. Number three.'

'Then I think we'd better be on our way there now, Crosby.'

Water Lane, Luston was one of the more insalubrious parts of that unattractive industrial town. It fronted the canal and consisted of a row of small terraced cottages, most of which had been subjected to half-hearted attempts at gentrification since the lock-keepers had moved out. Between them and the edge of the canal was a paved area where once there had been a towpath wide enough for horses. In front of some of the cottages were tubs full of flowering shrubs doing duty as make-shift gardens where there was no soil.

There were no tubs outside number three.

And answer came there none to polite knocking or, after that, to more importunate police knocking. The only response was from the house next door. A woman with hair dyed a fierce mahogany colour put her head round her front door and said if they were from the Social Security they'd be lucky getting him in there to come to the door at this hour of the day.

Detective Inspector Sloan said they weren't exactly from Social Security, although privately sometimes these days he wondered himself. More and more of the jobs that the police had to do now were definitely more social than security.

'He never opens up until it's dark,' the woman said. 'And then not always.'

'Light hurt his eyes, then?' asked Crosby.

She stared at his naivety. 'Too spaced-out to talk,' said the woman. 'And if you were to ask me, he doesn't want anyone to see his poor arms. His veins are black and blue.'

'Up to speed, is he?' asked Crosby.

She gave him another searching look. 'Gone past speed long ago,' she said tersely.

'Ah,' murmured Sloan. 'Like that, is it?'

The woman pointed towards the canal. 'It's a wonder to me that he hasn't gone in the water over there when he's been like that.'

'Is he in work?' asked Sloan.

'Work?' she croaked. 'That's rich, that is. He hasn't done a hand's turn since he's been here.'

'And where would he be getting the money from for drugs?' said Detective Inspector Sloan.

She shrugged. 'Where do any of them get the money?' she asked rhetorically. 'But they do, somehow, from somewhere. Do anything for it, of course.'

Sloan tried to look ingratiating. 'Do you happen to have his key by any chance? And his permission to use it, of course,' he added as a belated concession to the proprieties.

'Key? You don't need a key to get in there. The door's never locked and it's half off its hinges anyway.' She gave a high cackle. 'And believe you me, there's nothing in there to steal.'

Sloan gave another loud knock on Peter Caversham's door for form's sake and then pushed it gently open. He called out Caversham's name as he and Crosby entered the cottage. The front door gave straight into the main room. Initially, he thought the darkened room – there was an old blanket hooked across the window doing duty as a curtain – was empty, but it wasn't. There was a half-made bed in the corner; and what at first sight looked like a bundle of blankets turned out to be a human form.

The two policemen advanced with care but there was no need. The sallow-faced man lying there, although still breathing shallowly, was totally unresponsive to sound and touch. On the floor beside the bed lay an empty hypodermic syringe, its plunger pushed home as far as it would go.

'Dead to the wide,' said Crosby.

'But not dead yet,' said Detective Inspector Sloan. The scene reminded him of nothing so much as the one in the famous painting by the Pre-Raphaelite Henry Wallis of the death of the poet Thomas Chatterton. A police lecturer had once used it to illustrate his talk on fraud and fakes.

Except that Chatterton had been depicted as dead and this man was living – or partly living.

'Get an ambulance,' he instructed Crosby wearily. 'We can't leave him here like this.'

Chapter Thirteen

Spotted

'Well, Sloan,' barked Superintendent Leeyes, 'everything cut and dried now?'

'Not quite yet, sir.' Touching base – when that base was the police station at Berebury – was never an entirely unmitigated blessing. He took a deep breath and said, 'But we're working on it.'

'Good, good. Then, when you've cleared up the murder of this girl, you can get back to dealing with that heroin consignment.'

'It may not be as simple as that, sir.' He explained that they now knew that Whimbrel House was part of the drug scene.

'Not the boyfriend?' Leeyes sounded disappointed.

'We don't have any definite evidence as yet either way as to that, sir.'

'Circumstantial will do at a pinch,' said his superior officer with a fine disregard for the niceties of the law.

'As far as I can see, sir, there would have been no call for Colin Thornhill – that's the boyfriend – to go into Whimbrel House, eject a mummy from its case and put the girl in there instead,' said Sloan patiently, 'and then tell the coroner about it, when he could have just dumped her in the woods somewhere instead. She could have been missing for months if he had, and the trail gone cold.' He drew breath. 'But we'll be running some drug tests on him anyway.'

'Murder is bizarre,' pronounced Leeyes grandly. The superintendent gave one of his prodigious frowns. 'You never know where you are with either murder or drugs, Sloan. Remember that. No two manifestations are ever quite the same.'

'All drug dealers are nothing more than human vampires,' said Sloan heatedly, the image of Peter Caversham still with him. He knew that not all murderers were: quite often the Family Support Officers would report back to those investigating the crime that the real victim was the individual who had committed the murder – someone driven to do their nearest and dearest to death by the very person whom they'd killed.

The superintendent came back smartly with the observation that detachment was an important part of police professionalism and that Sloan shouldn't ever forget it.

'Drug dealers are bloodsuckers who make people dependent on them, sir; and then exploit their victims mercilessly until they haven't a drop of blood left in their veins or a penny in the bank,' said Sloan unrepentantly. He had been struck suddenly by the dealers' resemblance to the ichneumon fly but decided not to mention it.

'You can touch bottom very quickly on some substances,' conceded the superintendent, who only had a second gin and tonic at the golf club on Sunday mornings if it was offered to him by someone else.

'But heroin's the quickest by far,' said Sloan, explaining about Peter Caversham. 'We shall need to interview him when he's . . .' Sloan paused, casting about in his mind for the right word.

'No use putting "him in the longboat 'till he's sober" then?' interrupted Leeyes, on an unusually jovial note.

'Sentient,' finished Detective Inspector Sloan triumphantly. 'But it may be some time before he comes round and rejoins the human race. I've asked the local people there to keep an eye if he wakes up and walks out of the hospital.'

The superintendent said he was glad to hear it. 'It wouldn't do for ill to befall the man, Sloan, while there is an investigation in progress.'

'No, sir.' He hesitated. 'He may have been picked out as a suitable victim . . . Selected to be turned into an addict, I mean.'

'This Peter Caversham?'

'He had a sporting chance of inheriting the Caversham estate,' said Sloan. 'And he may have been the one who steered the drugs people to the empty house.' All the options would have to be explored. That was what police work was about.

'Money talks,' said Leeyes elliptically.

'We don't know whether he knew about it being empty, since the colonel wouldn't have him anywhere near the place, or,' he added significantly, 'whether anyone else did, and if so, who.'

Leeyes grunted.

'It has been established, sir, that those likely to inherit big money become the especial targets of drug dealers.'

The superintendent nodded at this. 'They say the Earl of Ornum has kicked his eldest son into touch.'

'Sir?'

'Stopped him inheriting a penny until he's twenty-five.'

'So,' said Sloan drily, 'all he has to do is to stay clean until then.'

'We can only hope,' the superintendent added with heavy irony, 'that he went to the right school.'

'I dare say the pushers pick out their prey quite as carefully as a stalking tiger does,' said Sloan. 'With no holds barred.'

Leeyes drummed his fingers on his desk. 'And in the meantime?'

'In the meantime, sir, I have put the rose bushes in tubs on the patio outside the back of my house in full view of anyone who cares to take a look over the back fence, and told – that is asked – my wife to accept any further deliveries that come.'

'That's all you can do, Sloan.' One winter the superintendent had attended an adult education class on Twentieth-Century British Prime Ministers. For some unfathomable reason it had been Herbert Henry Asquith who had taken his fancy. He had quoted the great man's favourite remark ever since. He did so now. 'Wait and see.'

'And told my wife to accept any other deliveries that

may come,' repeated Sloan, 'but not on any account to open them.'

'We have a few more questions further to our inquiries into the death of Jill Carter,' Detective Inspector Sloan announced with a certain formality at the offices of Pearson, Worrow and Gisby. 'We should like to see both partners.'

Detective Constable Crosby was quite taken aback when they were shown into the firm's interview room. 'Better than ours, sir.'

'It's the carpet that does it,' murmured Sloan absently.

The two accountants reached the room together, both professing a willingness to help the police with their inquiries in any way they could. But naturally, they insisted.

Sloan was well aware that normal police custom and practice – let alone PACE rules – held that persons being interviewed should be accompanied by their legal adviser and no one else; and certainly not be spoken to together with someone else who was also due to be questioned. This was because, when two or more persons were involved in an inquiry, the resulting separate statements could then be compared for any disparities.

It was what his mother, that staunch churchwoman, always called the 'Susannah and the elders method, dear'.

Like the Prophet Daniel in the Apocrypha, the

detective branch were great on spotting disparities between witness statements. Disparities led the police straight to what their press office always called 'Further inquiries', which was public relations-speak for: Watch this space: more to come.

There was another school of thought, though, and Sloan belonged to it: question two people at the same time about the same thing and tensions arose. Palpable tensions could sometimes be very significant.

'There are things we need to know,' he began now.

This was not an official interview.

Yet.

This was the police seeking information. And this was one detective inspector very anxious indeed to observe the byplay between two men, and a detective constable not interested in anything very much. The partners were two men one or both of whom might just possibly know a great deal more about: the late Jill Carter; a consignment of heroin that had fallen into official hands; a drug addict called Peter Caversham; or even the Lake Ryrie Project in the faraway Kingdom of Lasserta.

Detective Inspector Sloan was prepared to concede that it was equally possible that one man knew and the other man might suspect, but not know, something about one or all of these. And either man, though he did not himself know about any of these things, might perhaps suspect that his partner did.

That might emerge, too.

Sloan began his questions with the Lake Ryrie Project, and was aware that both accountants immediately relaxed. It wasn't anything at Lake Ryrie then, that they had been expecting the two policemen to come to see them about.

'Yes,' said Jim Pearson, looking puzzled. 'We audit the British end of their balance sheet – such as it is. We only charge them a nominal fee. They're one of Howard Air's good causes; he does a lot of charity work.'

'Theirs is one of the accounts our David Barton has always handled, but he's been out of action since his car accident,' put in Nigel Worrow, manifestly untroubled. 'I expect it's one of the little jobs that poor Jill picked up when she came to us. She was only a trainee, you know, so she only had small accounts to handle.'

'Not a lot of money involved in the Lake Ryrie Project anyway, in spite of Howard Air's best efforts,' said Jim Pearson, dismissively. 'People would rather give to the Animal Rescue place at Edsway. They like to see where their money's going.'

'I don't blame them,' came in Detective Constable Crosby, stoutly. His own early contacts with human cupidity had left him surprised at how many people took financial matters on trust.

'I rather think I signed them off myself,' said Worrow vaguely. 'Can't be sure, though.'

'How does the actual money get out there?' asked Sloan.

'Oh, the Calleford and County Bank'll do all that for them,' said Pearson. 'No problem.'

'They'll do the conversion from sterling into that odd currency they have out there easily enough,' supplemented his partner. 'I can't remember what it is . . .'

'Lemps,' said Jim Pearson, still visibly untroubled.

'We will obviously need a list of all clients whose accounts Jill Carter was working on.' Detective Inspector Sloan shifted his ground, seeking another, more sensitive area to probe.

'No problem,' repeated Jim Pearson helpfully. 'We didn't put any of the really difficult stuff her way, of course, just the routine, run-of-the-mill accounts.'

'The bread-and-butter ones,' agreed Worrow.

'Is there anything else you need, Inspector?' asked Pearson.

'Whatever you have on record about Peter Caversham,' said Sloan, his eyes apparently studiously downcast. They weren't so downcast though for him to be unaware of the reaction he'd provoked. On the contrary.

Worrow stiffened at once and exchanged a swift glance with his partner. 'That's quite different, Inspector. We'd have to have our client's say-so before we disclosed anything about his finances to anyone.' He appealed to his partner. 'Wouldn't we, Jim?'

'That or a court order, Inspector,' said Jim Pearson, suddenly more formal himself. 'We couldn't agree to a fishing expedition.'

'You wouldn't happen to have Horace Boller on your books, by any chance, would you?' asked Crosby, out of the blue.

'The boatman at Edsway?' Nigel Worrow gave a hollow laugh. 'Not likely. I shouldn't think he's got two pennies to rub together.'

'Oh, I don't know . . .' objected his partner. 'It would

never surprise me if old Horace hadn't got a nest egg somewhere. Appearances can be deceptive.'

'Not him, Jim, surely . . .'

'Mind you.' Pearson grimaced. 'I don't see him as a taxpayer, somehow.'

Worrow essayed a thin smile. 'Not his style, I grant you.'

Two of the many things Detective Inspector Sloan had learned in a long career in the police force were that the chemistry of social interaction wasn't deceptive, and that body language seldom lied. Even the ancients knew that. The Pinocchio effect – the nose that lengthened with each succeeding lie – had been founded on fact, after all. The nose did swell when a man lied. Antihistamines or something. So that medieval headpiece with the long nose, reserved for liars, had been grounded in pure and simple observation by his detective antecedents. He pulled himself together.

Nigel Worrow hadn't liked what Jim Pearson had said about Horace Boller one little bit, and neither Nigel Worrow nor Jim Pearson had relished any mention at all of Peter Caversham.

On the way back to the police station Sloan idly asked Crosby what he had made of the firm of Pearson, Worrow and Gisby.

'I bet that they even charge you for sneezing,' said that detective constable, oblivious to undercurrents and hidden agendas alike.

Chapter Fourteen

Used

'I think, sir, we might be beginning to make some headway.' Detective Inspector Sloan had sought out Superintendent Leeyes at the earliest possible moment to make his report.

'At long last, Sloan,' said Superintendent Leeyes, never one to award verbal rosettes for anything less than conviction and sentence – and preferably a long sentence at that – in the Crown Court.

'That is, sir, we may just be getting near enough to the truth to be frightening someone.'

'Good, good,' said the superintendent heartily. 'Fear is always a factor in murder, Sloan. And it can be a factor for good, too, don't forget.'

'Sir?'

'There's healthy fear. You've only to look at the death threats you get from doctors these days.'

Sloan placed the source of this accusation quite easily: straight to the superintendent's paunch, to the size of which the police doctor had lately taken great exception.

'You see, sir,' he said, averting his gaze from his

superior officer's burgeoning girth, 'my wife tells me we've just had another special delivery at home.'

Leeyes grunted. 'So someone's hoping you'll settle for the ha'pence rather than the kicks?'

'For a bit more than ha'pence,' said Sloan feelingly.

'What is it this time? More roses?'

'Tickets for two on a special luxury tour of the great gardens of Europe, no extras.'

'They know your weak spots, don't they?' growled Leeyes.

'It's the trip we always planned to take when I retired,' he said with dignity.

'So someone's done their homework, Sloan.'

'Paid for in cash at the travel company's head office,' he said, 'for a Mr and Mrs C. D. Sloan of Berebury.'

'Hitting where it hurts,' mused Leeyes. He lifted a bushy eyebrow at an angle that Wayne Goddard would have envied.

'It's seeing the gardens I – we – would have been going for,' insisted Sloan. 'Not the luxury.'

'Quite right,' said Leeyes, adding obscurely, 'The nuts come when the teeth have gone.'

'Yes, sir. Another interesting thing is that this tour leaves the country first thing Monday morning.'

'And so,' concluded Leeyes weightily, 'some person or persons unknown are indicating they very much hoped that you would be on it.'

'And thus off their backs,' said Sloan.

The superintendent drummed his fingers on the top of his desk. 'Which must mean, Sloan, that you are a bit nearer the mark than you think.'

'I can see the significance of that, sir,' admitted Sloan. 'But what I can't see is in what way I – that is we – might be near anything.'

He was still smarting from an encounter with the toffee-nosed senior partner of Ickham and Grove, Chartered Accountants of St Matthew's Court, Berebury. Entering their discreetly opulent offices had had a lot in common with arriving at the reception counter of a five-star hotel. Christian names had not been bandied about by staff or anyone else. 'Howard Air's accountants, sir, assure us that all their clients are men and women of unimpeachable probity.'

'No such thing,' came back Leeyes smartly. 'Everyone's got their price.'

'And that they, Ickham and Grove that is, would not be auditing them if they weren't.'

'That's unnatural for a start,' said Leeyes, ever the police officer.

'Moreover, sir, their senior partner assured me that Howard Air's business and private accounts demonstrated him to be an astute, hard-working and successful businessman.'

'You'd think he'd be clever enough to be on the fiddle, then,' said Leeyes unfairly, 'wouldn't you?'

'And that's quite apart from his local political and charitable works.'

'He's not on the Town Council Planning Committee, I hope, Sloan?' said Leeyes. 'Lead us not into temptation, and all that.'

'No, sir. Just Museums and Amenities.'

The superintendent wasn't interested in Museums and Amenities.

'And Ickham and Grove are quite happy for us to examine any or all of Air's accounts, provided they have his consent.'

'Hrrrmph.'

'They could see no reason for this to be withheld.' The auditors had insisted to Sloan that Mr Air was always very helpful and cooperative. They had signally failed, though, to smile at the inspector's pointing out the biblical connection with their address. The remark that Matthew had been a tax gatherer had provoked no response at all.

'Which means that there's nothing to be found there,' said Leeyes dismissively. 'Now, what is to be done about this continental trip you've had the tickets for?'

This was something that had been taxing Sloan.

'I thought, sir, if my wife were to do some shopping for new summer dresses the word might get around.'

'Good thinking.'

'And perhaps some extra photographic film. The camera shop man is a great gossip. She could chat him up: tell him we were off and so forth.'

'But nothing to come out of our imprest account,' rejoined Leeyes spiritedly when he mentioned this.

'No, sir. Out of mine.' He coughed. 'There's something else . . .'

'Well?'

'Ought I to book myself off duty for Monday?'

The atmosphere in the room changed on the instant

and the superintendent began to look every year of his age. 'The enemy within?'

'One can't be too careful.'

'Even police station walls have ears,' said Leeyes, more melancholy than Sloan had ever known him before, 'especially where drugs are concerned.'

'These people, whoever they are, do seem so very omniscient.'

'That's the trouble with drug dealing. It doesn't follow the rules. Remember that.'

'Which doesn't make our job any easier,' said Sloan feelingly.

'It isn't an easy job to begin with. You should know that by now, Sloan.'

'Yes, sir.'

'By the way, has Crosby's contribution amounted to very much?' asked the superintendent, rapidly regaining his usual aplomb. 'Since you seem to be acknowledging his existence by the use of the plural.'

'Not yet,' said Sloan tersely. He'd quite forgotten for the moment the class on English grammar once attended by the superintendent. 'But there's always the hope that he'll come up with something.'

Leeyes grunted again.

'On the other hand,' persisted Sloan, 'with whoever's trying to bribe me . . .'

'Before they put the frighteners on,' interrupted Leeyes, true Job's comforter. 'That'll come next, Sloan, and don't say you haven't been warned.'

' . . . there is also the very real possibility,' continued

Sloan, 'that they might be wanting to put me off doing the next thing I had planned.'

'And what is that, might I ask?'

'Searching the Calleshire Animal Rescue Centre at Edsway, sir. I got a quick look at it while I was over there.'

'Possibilities?'

'There's a dozen places and more where you could easily hide up any amount of drugs as soon as they were got ashore.' He wrinkled his nose at the memory of the animal sanctuary. 'And however much they smelt, no one would be any the wiser.'

'Boller goes there every day,' mused Leeyes, 'and that accountant fellow Worrow sails off Edsway most weekends, you said.'

Sloan nodded. 'But what I really want to be let known, sir, and reported in the newspapers as soon as possible, is that Colin Thornhill . . .'

'The boyfriend?'

' . . . is here at the police station helping us with our inquiries.'

'They looked like policemen to me, Mr Caversham,' said the woman with the mahogany-coloured hair from next door.

The man on the bed muttered something.

Unwashed, unshaven and barely properly clothed, something intangible which she couldn't begin to define still stopped her addressing this wreck of a man by his Christian name. She said, 'You can always tell with policemen, can't you?'

The man looked at her blankly with narrowed pupils.

'Policemen,' she repeated. 'Before you were taken into hospital.'

He stirred as if movement hurt him.

'They came to see you yesterday,' she said.

He groaned as if it was not movement now but reality that was painful.

'I told them the door was open,' she said apologetically. 'I know I needn't have done but they could have always got a warrant, couldn't they?' The people who lived down by the canal were wise, worldly-wise, in their generation from bitter experience.

He made a sound that might have been agreement.

'They looked at you,' she said, not unkindly, 'and then they went away.'

He groaned again, his adulterated mind slowly returning from wherever it had been while under the influence of heroin.

'You'll feel better soon,' his neighbour said, knowing it to be untrue. He'd been happier, much happier, in that nirvana which lay well beyond the Land of Nod. It was the here and now which held no attractions for Peter Caversham by comparison, and very well she – and he – knew it.

He tried to hitch himself up on an elbow but fell back on the bed at his first attempt. His second effort was more successful, although it appeared that the world as seen from this perspective was no better than when he had been lying down. He showed signs of resuming his supine position but his neighbour stopped him by deftly inserting a pillow behind his shoulders.

'Ah . . .' Peter Caversham let out the sound almost as if it was an involuntary response.

It was enough for his neighbour. 'You'll be able to manage something to drink then,' she said, going off to the kitchen. 'That's if I can find anything here fit for a dog to drink,' she muttered to herself. 'If not, it'll have to be water.'

Water it was. Getting the sallow-faced man to drink it proved more difficult. More experienced in these matters than she would have cared to admit, the woman brought the water to him not in a cup or a glass tumbler but in a small milk jug. She stood over Peter Caversham as if he was a child while he raised his damp and shaking hands to the lip of the jug and drank.

His furred tongue moistened, the capacity for speech seemed to return to him. 'God, I feel awful.'

'You smell awful, too,' said his neighbour, stepping back as the man's offensive breath struck her nostrils. 'Ughhh . . .'

He ignored this. 'The post, has it come?'

She brought his letters to him. He riffled urgently through them, fighting all the time to overcome his tremor. He was seeking the one that mattered to him most, the thin brown envelope with the benefit money in it that he needed so badly. He quickly found the one he wanted and tore it open with fumbling fingers, not bothering at all with a thick cream envelope addressed to Peter Caversham, Esquire.

That envelope wasn't thin and brown. It was made of very good quality paper indeed and carried the address of the offices of Messrs Puckle, Puckle and Nunnery, Solicitors and Notaries Public of Berebury, on the back.

He did not even turn it over.

Chapter Fifteen

Hinge Cracked

'I reckon we're just going round in circles now, sir,' said Detective Constable Crosby gloomily, plonking a pile of folders heavily down on Sloan's desk. 'This lot is from Pearson, Worrow and Gisby: the files of all the clients that the deceased had been working on, as we requested.'

'That's our next job, Crosby,' Sloan said bracingly. 'You'll have to get cracking with your calculator.'

The detective constable sniffed. 'Not that those accountant people are ever going to send us anything worthwhile, anyway, are they, sir? Not them; they're not that silly.'

'Not anything that they have reason to believe is worthwhile,' agreed Detective Inspector Sloan, scrupulously exact.

His private perception of his own small office always swung wildly from that of sanctum to that of bed of nails. Crosby's mere arrival – let alone his pessimism – had sent it straight to the latter category.

'But they may not know, Crosby . . .' He reached his hand out. 'Let me see the Lake Ryrie balance sheet anyway. It's the only name we know at the moment.'

Crosby flipped his way through a pile of folders and extracted one. 'Here you are, sir. Annual accounts of the Lake Ryrie Reserve, Lasserta.'

Sloan opened it without any idea of what to look for. He almost lost interest when he found he was considering a set of statements of an account which showed under a thousand pounds as having been transmitted to Lasserta in the last financial year.

'That,' he said, 'is not a hill of beans these days. I reckon we can tick that one off. I don't think we really need to worry about the grand total of £947 sent to Lasserta last year.'

Crosby wasn't interested in figures but he remained gloomy. 'I reckon that just at this minute, sir, there's more that we don't know about this girl's murder than what we do . . .'

'More people always know Tom Fool, Crosby.'

'For starters,' continued Crosby morosely, ignoring this last, 'we don't even know why Jill Carter was killed yet . . .'

'No.'

' . . . unless it was by her other half, and then in that case I suppose we don't need to.'

'That remark, Crosby, is a sad indictment of either your sex education or your constable's training, or both.'

'Sir?'

'Forget it,' said Sloan immediately. 'Remember instead that nor do we know why the coroner was told about her death. Or why he was told in the stirring-up manner he was.'

'No, sir.'

'And that's the oddest thing of all, that is. Doesn't make sense.'

Crosby said, 'And we don't know why her body was put in that mummy case in Whimbrel House in the first place.'

'Not even that,' agreed Sloan. He added mildly, 'Actually, Crosby, we don't need to know why she was killed or why she was put in the case. We just need to know who by.'

'Yes, sir,' he said.

'Assuming both actions to have been taken by one and the same person or persons.'

The detective constable wasn't listening. 'And then there's all these drugs . . .'

'They haven't gone away,' concurred Sloan solemnly, 'although some of them are now safe in the arms of our friends the Customs and Excise.'

'But, sir, we don't know yet for sure whether drugs've got anything to do with the girl's murder . . .'

'Or everything to do with it,' pointed out Sloan. 'Since there was heroin where she and the mummy came from.'

' . . . even though heroin had obviously got a lot to do with the dreadful state of that man who was so completely spaced-out in Luston,' said Crosby censoriously. 'Peter Caversham.'

'At the mention of whose name Jim Pearson and Nigel Worrow shut up like a pair of Horace Boller's clams,' remarked Sloan.

'And as for him . . .'

'Who? Oh, Horace Boller.' Detective Inspector Sloan

gave an unexpected grin. 'I dare say we'll all go to our graves without knowing everything he's been up to. But, rest assured, Crosby, Customs and Excise have his every movement taped.'

'That's something, sir.'

'But not a lot when you're as wily as our Horace.'

'I suppose not, sir.' He turned and rose as there was a tap on the door. He came back reading from a message sheet in his hand. 'I don't believe it . . .'

'What, Crosby?' Detective Inspector Sloan watched as the detective constable stood stock-still in the middle of the office floor.

Whatever Sloan had been expecting it wasn't this.

'We have just had a reply from vehicle registrations at Swansea about that Bentley we saw in the museum car park.'

'And?'

'And it doesn't belong to Howard Air.'

'No?'

'It's registered in the name of Marcus Alan George Fixby-Smith.'

'It is, is it?' Sloan sat back in his chair. 'Well, well, I wonder what his story will be?'

'Must have cost a bomb,' offered Crosby.

'Money doesn't mean anything in the drugs world,' said Sloan, newly primed. 'The only problem the dealer has is how to use it without it showing too much and getting noticed.'

'Classic Bentleys show,' insisted Crosby. The detective constable was only able to balance his own meagre finances with much contriving. He said, as one propounding a simple fact, 'That's why people have them.'

'If Fixby-Smith is caught up in the drugs racket,' said Sloan, thinking aloud, 'it would explain the letter to the coroner that made sure the mummy case was opened there and not at Whimbrel House.' This was something that he still couldn't understand.

Crosby frowned. 'I reckon that's one of life's little mysteries.'

'That's only if someone wanted us to be sure of finding it at the museum.'

'And nowhere else,' contributed the detective constable.

Sloan frowned. 'They – whoever they are – might have thought they could keep tabs on what was discovered there.'

'Perhaps they just didn't want it found at Whimbrel House, sir.'

'That, too,' he agreed. Perhaps Crosby was learning to think at last. 'Anything else?'

Crosby screwed up his brow in thought. 'Or needed to control exactly when it was found.'

Sloan gave a quick nod. 'Timing seems to have been of the essence, although I can't quite make out why yet. Not for certain, anyway.'

Detective Constable Crosby sighed. 'Like they say, sir. There are only two things in the world that are certain: death and taxes.'

*

'Fascinating, quite fascinating, Inspector,' declared Professor Miles Upton, rubbing his hands. 'I am happy to see that Rodoheptah is in such an excellent state of preservation.'

'Really?' said Sloan politely. He was looking down over the top of a surgical mask at what seemed to him a confused jumble of petrified coconut matting. Even looked at more closely, it didn't appear like flesh at all. More like old and worn brown leather.

'A first-class example of its period.' The palaeopathologist, who was clearly an enthusiast as well as a specialist, peered happily at the remains on the mortuary slab.

From what Sloan could see over the top of the detective constable's mask, Crosby looked as dubious as he himself felt.

'That should make your own work more interesting,' said Sloan civilly. The condition of the mummy didn't make it more interesting for him. He didn't care how the man called Rodoheptah had met his end. Crime at Ra'fan – then or now – was not his problem.

Who had killed Jill Carter was his problem.

And why.

And why her body had been sent round to the museum in place of the poor muddled agglomeration of posthumous fragments that should have been delivered there. And where Mr Granville Locombe-Stableford, HM Coroner for East Calleshire, came into the picture.

If he did.

Whether the Kirk sisters' late nephew Derek had

come into a very large sum of money in cash dis-
honestly or not was his problem, too.

And so was the identity of the person for whom that
consignment of heroin in Horace Boller's lobster creel
had been meant. And exactly how the money which the
sale of that selfsame heroin would have generated could
have found its way into the legitimate local economy.

But his most pressing problem was finding out
exactly who had responded so speedily to the signal on
his patio that bribery might divert or even halt his,
Sloan's, proper investigation. It was a presumption for
which someone somewhere would have to pay very
heavily or he, Detective Inspector Sloan, upholder of
the peace, would know the reason why.

'What would really help,' the Professor was saying,
'is a CT scan.'

'Computed tomography would be very useful,'
agreed Dr Dabbe, one professional to another.

'But I'll do an endoscopy first,' said Professor Upton,
turning to his black bags. He produced a long black
flexible tube. 'I expect you've got a fibre optic light
source and monitor here somewhere.'

Dr Dabbe said that equipment wasn't a problem.

'Don't worry, anybody,' said the professor. 'It's mini-
mally invasive.'

Detective Constable Crosby might have been
masked but the doctor must still have seen his rolling
eyes because he added reassuringly, 'We use an industrial instrument for this, not a human one.'

Crosby looked anything but reassured as the two
doctors inserted the thick tube through what remained

of the mummy's mouth, peering at the screen withal. This venture into the interior showed a confused picture that meant nothing to Sloan.

'Gets to the parts other beers don't reach, doesn't it?' said Crosby uneasily.

'Ah,' said Dr Dabbe at one point. 'Do you see that? There. I've always found the jejunum empty at death.'

'I'll do a biopsy there,' said Miles Upton. 'And down here.'

'Now, that's interesting, too.' Dr Dabbe pointed to the screen.

'What would that be?' enquired Sloan.

'Not my field, Sloan,' said Dr Dabbe, 'but it looks remarkably like *Anobium punctatum* to me.'

'Sounds nasty,' said Crosby from the sidelines.

'Adult woodworm,' said Miles Upton.

'A lot of it about,' said Dabbe in much the same way as did doctors to the living.

'We'll be getting some of the histological sections from these tissues rehydrated and processed. Then, Inspector, we'll be able to tell you more,' said Professor Upton in much the same way as Dr Dabbe usually did.

The arrival of the police search party at the Calleshire Animal Sanctuary at Edsway produced nothing but an open invitation to look wherever they wanted.

Jennifer Kirk waved a hand round the place and added with a rough laugh that they could do whatever they liked as long as they didn't frighten the horses.

'Thank you, miss,' said Crosby primly. 'We shan't be doing that.'

'Something has,' she retorted. 'They've been very unsettled all day today.'

'And the dogs,' said her sister.

'Horace been here yet?' asked Sloan.

Alison shook her head. 'He's tidal, is Horace. But he'll be along, never worry.'

'Would you be looking for anything in particular?' asked Jennifer as the men got ready.

'We're just trying to make sure that nobody's been using your premises for something they didn't ought to,' said Detective Crosby colloquially. 'While your backs are turned, of course,' he added hastily, catching a glint in the elder Miss Kirk's eye.

Jennifer nodded her comprehension. 'I can tell you one thing and that's if there's any funny business going on round here, we don't know about it.'

'And we'd tell you if we did,' said Alison Kirk flatly.

Jennifer gave an earthy chuckle. 'We wouldn't be as skint as we are if we weren't more honest than most. Now, then, where do you and your people want to start?'

Detective Inspector Sloan stationed himself outside the back door of the house and watched as his men fanned out over the animal sanctuary.

'Tell 'em to look out for the swan,' advised Jennifer Kirk at his elbow. 'It may have a broken wing but the other one's in excellent working order.'

'And not to let the badger out,' said her sister. 'He's not well enough to go back to the wood yet, poor thing.'

'Old Brock's one of our success stories,' remarked

Jennifer Kirk. 'We thought he was beyond aid when they brought him here, but with a bit more tender loving care he'll be as right as rain again in another week or two.'

Sloan wasn't really listening. He was watching. Which was how he noticed the changed demeanour of Detective Constable Crosby as he emerged from the shed that sheltered Dunce the donkey. He hadn't got straw behind his ears, but there was plenty round his boots and he was still clutching an absurd handful of the stuff.

The constable was trying to shout something to Sloan as he ran across the yard, but whatever it was was drowned by the braying of the donkey which was now cantering companionably along by the policeman's side.

'Sir,' he said breathlessly. 'Sir, can you come? I'm afraid we've found . . . something.'

'Something?'

'Someone,' he said urgently. 'Under the donkey's straw.' Crosby jerked his shoulder away as Dunce gave him a playful nip. 'Get off! No, not you, sir, the donkey. This way, sir. Mind your head. You'll have to bend it to get in. And it's a bit dark. Look there, sir. Over in the corner.'

The person lying half under the straw was, unlike Brock the badger, not only beyond human aid but beyond tender loving care as well.

Well beyond.

And he wasn't going to be as right as rain again.

Ever.

'Wayne Goddard,' said Detective Constable Crosby.

'Last seen alive by us slipping out of the Ornum Arms,' said Detective Inspector Sloan sombrely.

'And who helped Sid Wetherspoon move the mummy from Whimbrel House to the museum,' said Crosby.

Chapter Sixteen

Backstrip Missing

'Same song, second verse, I take it, Sloan,' commented Superintendent Leeyes when the news was relayed to him.

'Yes, sir,' agreed Detective Inspector Sloan, deeply conscious of failure. One of the primary objects of catching murderers was to stop them repeating the exercise.

'The missing link, you might say.'

'The death of Wayne Goddard would seem to link up with Jill Carter's murder,' said Sloan cautiously. 'Although it is not clear how.'

'And are we to suppose that when Wayne Goddard visited Whimbrel House in the course of his employment, he noticed something to do with drugs had been going on there . . .'

'I think that is part of the story,' began Sloan in measured tones. 'But only part.'

' . . . and was unwise enough to act on what he had seen?'

'A distinct possibility, sir. It would account for his swift elimination.' Sloan didn't really like using gangland language but it fitted this scenario only too well.

'The trouble with this case,' said Leeyes profoundly, 'is that there are no lines in the sand.'

'The rules don't seem to apply to drug dealers,' said Sloan, answering the thought rather than his superior's words. 'Or drug takers, come to that.' Sometimes there was a distinction between the two; sometimes there wasn't. Some of the takers dealt, some of the dealers took. But not all. It was pretty nearly certain that Mr Big, the man the police wanted most of all, didn't take drugs. Mr Big would need all his wits about him . . . all the time.

'It's the old, old, story,' said Leeyes sapiently. 'One gains and the other loses.'

Sloan nodded. In his book Peter Caversham was one of the losers. Even if he were to inherit the Caversham settled estate.

'But none of this explains the death of the girl,' said Leeyes. 'She was a loser.'

'Or where the Kirk nephew's money came from,' said Sloan. He wouldn't like to have to say whether Derek had been a winner or a loser.

'Or the museum curator's Bentley,' said Leeyes thoughtfully. 'They were always a good car, you know, Sloan.'

'Or,' said Sloan, ignoring this tempting byway and coming to the nub of the matter, 'how the drug money is laundered; but I intend to find out.'

'Good.'

'And exactly who it is,' said Detective Inspector Sloan, with quite a different note coming into his voice, 'who has been trying to bribe me.'

'Mouths have been stopped with gold before now, Sloan, even police ones,' Leeyes said. 'You've been posted as being on annual leave from Monday. And Sloan . . .'

'Sir?'

'Watch your step,' said the superintendent gruffly.

'Don't just do something, Crosby,' commanded Sloan quixotically as he came back from talking to the superintendent. 'Sit there.'

The constable sat down.

'And think.'

'Yes, sir.' This was clearly proving more difficult for him because, instead, Crosby glanced repeatedly across the yard of the animal sanctuary to where one police officer was methodically erecting tape barriers round the place where the body had been found and another was standing on guard outside the donkey's stable, keeping out all and sundry. The second man's only challenge was coming from the donkey. Dunce was making it clear with nips and tugs that he did not like being kept out of his own domain.

'Something here doesn't add up,' said Sloan.

'No, sir.'

'Wayne Goddard was at Whimbrel House this week,' said Sloan. 'Probably more than once.'

'Tuesday and Thursday,' said Crosby, adding conscientiously, 'that we know about. He may have been there other times, too.'

'And we have evidence that Whimbrel House was

being used as a distribution centre for drugs – most probably heroin coming ashore at Edsway.'

'So Scenes of Crimes say, sir.' He sniffed. 'Scenes of two crimes, you might say.'

'Although we don't know yet whether the heroin landed off Edsway was parked somewhere here at the sanctuary *en route* for Whimbrel House.'

'Nice and handy, if it was,' remarked Crosby.

'Which could have happened quite easily without Alison or Jennifer Kirk knowing about it.'

'Easily,' agreed Crosby. 'It's near enough to the shore to bring it on foot.'

'And we still haven't discovered how the Kirk sisters' nephew Derek got his hands on that cash,' murmured Sloan.

The Kirk sisters had retreated to their kitchen and the teapot. Today, someone else was watching out for the arrival of Horace Boller and his fish.

'Derek died this week,' Crosby reminded him.

'Now Wayne's been murdered, too,' said Sloan pensively. He must do his thinking now, aware as he was that soon, very soon, there wouldn't be any time to think; not after the Scenes of Crime outfit and their various camp followers arrived at the animal sanctuary. Thought would very quickly give way to action then.

'Looks like it, sir. Not an accident, anyway, not from the looks of him.'

'Nothing's been an accident, Crosby.' Sloan stopped suddenly. 'Wait a minute, wait a minute. There's been one accident, hasn't there?' His old friend, Harry Harpe of Traffic Division, had been the first to tell him about

183

it: an accident to David Barton, the senior audit clerk of Pearson, Worrow and Gisby, Chartered Accountants, who had been lying unconscious in hospital ever since.

'Sir?'

'I'm still thinking, Crosby,' he said. And he was. Jill Carter had been given some of David Barton's work to do at Pearson, Worrow and Gisby; and she had been murdered even before Wayne Goddard. Derek, the wayward nephew, had merely died, but had become inexplicably and suddenly rich before he popped his clogs.

'Very well, sir.' The constable sat silent and still.

'Crosby,' said Sloan presently, 'do you remember saying that some professional people charge you even when you sneeze?'

'Yes, sir. There's nothing ever comes free from the dark suits brigade.'

'And naturally if they're going to charge you for something then they will have to make a note about it, won't they?' At some later date he would explore the semantic differences between the dark suits of Crosby's homespun philosophy and the black-coated workers so favoured in the terminology of the sociologists, but not now. There wasn't time.

'Yes, sir,' agreed the constable stolidly.

'Crosby, I think we'll have to pay Pearson, Worrow and Gisby another visit in the very very near future. Like now.'

*

'But it's Saturday morning, Inspector,' protested Jim Pearson. 'That's why I'm here at home. There's nobody in the office today.' He paused to listen. 'Yes, of course, there could be if I call staff in. Who? Nigel? No, not him. Yes, yes, Inspector, I quite understand that it's something important and that you wouldn't do it otherwise, but it's never any use trying to get hold of Nigel at the weekend. Why? Because he'll be at sea already, that's why. He always takes the *Berebury Belle* out first thing Saturday morning. I dare say he won't be back now until late tomorrow evening. Where's he gone? I don't know but he and his wife like exploring all the little inlets along the coast. Oh, all right, then, if you insist. I'll get straight in there. And my people?' He sighed audibly. 'Exactly who else do you want to talk to? The office manager and our telephonist. I'll see what I can do.'

Jim Pearson replaced the telephone receiver a very worried man indeed.

'I know it's a Saturday morning, Howard,' began Marcus Fixby-Smith plaintively, 'but do you think you could possibly come in to the museum today?'

'I expect I could if it was important,' sighed Howard Air wearily, 'though it's my morning for a lie-in and I'm still in bed. What's the problem now?'

'My aunt.'

'Your aunt?' echoed the other man cautiously. 'Marcus, this business with the girl and the mummy hasn't sent you off your head, has it?'

'I can't help it, Howard,' wailed the curator, 'if I had a rich aunt, can I?'

'No . . . no, I suppose not.' Howard coughed. 'Are you sure you're all right?'

'And I can't help it if she died and left me her precious old Bentley, can I?'

'No, but . . .' He had another burst of coughing.

'The police seemed to think I could have done,' said the curator unhappily. 'They said it was an aspirational car, whatever that might be.'

'Look here, Marcus, this isn't some ridiculous ploy to do with your favourite author, is it?' He coughed again. 'Because, if so, I think it's in pretty poor taste with that poor girl lying murdered in our mummy case.'

'Favourite author?' It was Fixby-Smith's turn to sound bewildered. Then he relaxed. 'Oh, you mean P. G. Wodehouse. No, no.'

'You told me he was into aunts.' Howard Air sounded breathless. 'I wouldn't know myself.'

'Nothing to do with him. It's the police,' he said hollowly. 'They didn't believe me when I told them my aunt left me the Bentley.'

'They can always check if they want to,' said Howard.

'And then,' quavered Fixby-Smith, 'they wanted to know where I'd been last night.'

'That's different,' said his chairman alertly. 'What happened last night?'

'I don't know,' said Fixby-Smith miserably. 'They wouldn't tell me, but it must have been something very serious because they took my fingerprints. And, Howard . . .'

'Yes?'

'I think I'm going to have to see my solicitor.'

'Why?' enquired Howard Air bluntly.

'The police asked me if I was taking drugs.' His voice rose almost an octave. 'Me!'

'And are you?' countered the businessman, a trifle maliciously.

'No, of course not.'

'Half Calleshire seems to be on one or the other of them so you can't blame the police for asking,' said Howard Air.

'But not me,' averred Marcus Fixby-Smith with unexpected emphasis. 'Drugs are for failures. And, anyway, they might affect my judgement.'

'That would never do, would it?' murmured the Chairman of the Museums and Amenities Committee. 'But, all the same, Marcus, I think you can handle this on your own. I'm up at four o'clock every weekday morning and I'm just not going to get up for you now. This time the Curator of the Greatorex Museum'll just have to manage as best he can without his committee chairman.'

'Traffic,' said a voice. 'Inspector Harpe speaking.'

'That you, Harry? Seedy here. Harry, that man you were telling me about: the one who was hit by another car at the crossroads who's still unconscious . . .'

'You mean David Barton?'

'That's him,' said Sloan. 'Tell me, has he been tested for drugs at the hospital?'

'And alcohol,' said the traffic man succinctly. 'Routine procedure these days after all road traffic accidents. No arguing with a blood test, you know.' He paused. 'It doesn't stop some of 'em from trying, though.'

'Well? What was the outcome?'

'No trace of either drugs or alcohol in him,' said 'Happy Harry' immediately. 'The other man was well over the drink limit, though. It'll be an open-and-shut case as soon as we can get to court with it.'

'Some people have all the luck,' said Sloan.

'What, me?' said Happy Harry indignantly. 'Let me tell you, Seedy, that I've been . . .'

'Some other time, Harry. Some other time.'

River Street, Berebury, was busier on a Saturday morning than on any weekday but Crosby still found parking the police car easy. There was no traffic warden in sight to say them nay when he drew the vehicle to a standstill outside the offices of Pearson, Worrow and Gisby.

Jim Pearson might have been the firm's senior partner but he made no fuss about being doorkeeper as well this morning.

'Cheryl's here, Inspector,' he said as he admitted them, 'and our office manager is on his way in.'

'Good, good,' said Sloan. 'Now, what I want to know is how your costing system works.'

Whatever question Pearson had been expecting, it wasn't this one. He looked blankly at the two policemen.

'When someone sneezes,' said Detective Constable Crosby, 'how does it get on their bill?'

'On a time basis,' said Pearson hastily.

'But how?' asked Detective Inspector Sloan.

'If it's on the telephone, then Cheryl, our girl on the switchboard, makes a note of the name called and that of the member of staff handling the query.'

'And?'

'And passes on that list on a daily basis to our office manager who costs it out according to the length of the conversation and the seniority of the person speaking at this end.'

'That's what we thought,' said Sloan. 'Now, what about internal calls?'

Pearson licked lips unaccountably dry. 'The senior of the two people talking takes the responsibility for booking out any charges to the client, should he or she think an additional cost appropriate.'

'What we want is a list of any telephone calls made or received by Jill Carter in the week before she was murdered.'

'No problem,' said Jim Pearson weakly. 'We should be able to pull them out easily enough.' He moistened his lips again. 'Was there any name in particular that you were looking out for?'

Sloan fell back on a time-honoured formula: 'I'm afraid that that is something I am not at liberty to discuss with you . . .'

' . . . at this stage.' Detective Constable Crosby completed Sloan's sentence after the manner born.

'Where to, now, sir?' asked Detective Constable Crosby, when they had emerged from the accountants' offices with several pieces of paper.

Sloan didn't answer.

After studying the list of telephone calls made in the course of her work by Jill Carter – only one was to Colin Thornhill and that presumably was in the course of true love, not accounts – Sloan sat for several minutes in the police car without saying a word. This was still parked outside the premises of Pearson, Worrow and Gisby, Chartered Accountants.

The Saturday shoppers eddied round the car like the ebb and flow of the tide at Edsway while Sloan sat and thought about fungible economies and the legitimization of money; about death and taxes; about one accident, one death from natural causes and two murders; and about one man nearly, but not quite, dead from heroin addiction.

Two small boys came up and stared at the two policemen, sitting silent in their car, and for a moment considered pulling faces at them but thought better of it and moved away again.

Sloan went on to think about more than one disturbance in the night at an animal sanctuary; about an animal reserve abroad whence came edible substances; and above all about the unlimited resources at the beck and call of the money-launderer.

There were some things which ready money couldn't buy, but there were also a lot of things that money and the promise of drugs could procure: odd things, such as a person to follow Jill Carter from her place of employment at short notice; and another stranger, or perhaps the same one, to invent a cock and bull story for the benefit of a public house landlord – and anyone else who might later care to enquire – about a quarrel over curtains that had never taken place.

And another to chat up his wife about the proclivities of one, Christopher Dennis Sloan.

Unlimited money could buy even odder things: such as an endowment insurance policy no longer of value to a dying policyholder but with considerable potential benefit to whomsoever owned it at the time of the policyholder's death, benefit in the way of the ability to convert suspect money in cash to funds with inbuilt probity: money-laundering, in fact.

And it could buy patio roses and superlative specialist holidays with a tailor-made significance to their recipients well beyond the substance.

He straightened up in the passenger seat and said, 'It's all right, Crosby. You can get going now.'

'Where to, sir?' The engine was purring on the instant.

'Back to the station for a search warrant.'

'Where for, sir?' He wheeled the car round in a tight circle against the traffic in a manoeuvre which, performed by anyone else, would have produced shaking fists from other motorists.

'For evidence,' said Detective Inspector Sloan.

Chapter Seventeen

Corners Blunted

'It was a couple of things that Crosby said, sir, that put me on to it.' Duty-bound, Sloan had reported to the superintendent as soon as he could.

'I don't believe it.' Leeyes sounded astounded. 'Crosby? About Howard Air?'

'No, sir. About money.'

'Crosby? Are you sure, Sloan?'

'First of all, sir, he said something about the professions even charging you for sneezing.'

'That's fair enough.' Leeyes snorted. 'Nothing too clever about that.'

'And then he repeated that old saying about death and taxes being the only things that are certain in life.'

'Benjamin Franklin.' Leeyes, autodidact, identified who had said that very swiftly.

'And when you started to think about it, sir, all Howard Air wanted to do was to pay tax on as much of his income as he could, and then it was safe from suspicion and sequestration.'

'Sounds funny to me,' said Leeyes.

'Laundered to perfection, in fact.' Air's actions met all the requirements that Jenny, the forensic accountant with the luscious voice, had laid down for a successful transformation of funds illegal, to funds absolutely respectable.

'And are you going to tell me how he did it, Sloan, or do I have to guess?' asked Leeyes acidly.

'He did it by sending money out to the Lake Ryrie Reserve in Lasserta.'

'That doesn't make it respectable.'

'No, sir, but what Howard Air did was send out money only ostensibly to the reserve. It didn't stay there. It went on to the fruit and vegetable growers of Lasserta.' It had been the ambassador, Anthony Heber-Hibbs, hadn't it, who had reckoned that a little corruption was good for an economy. He was probably right.

'I know, I know, Sloan, and you're going to tell me they sent it back cleaned and ironed.'

'Not quite, sir. The growers in Lasserta sent back fruit and vegetables in exchange but what they didn't send were any invoices for the goods.' This was something that he had already checked with Ickham and Grove, which staid firm had been shaken to the core by the perfidy of their client. They were busy explaining that someone wanting to pay more tax rather than less had been, until now, quite outside their experience.

Leeyes grunted.

'You see, sir, Howard Air's income was inflated, but his money was to all intents and purposes squeaky clean because of his having paid tax on it.'

'I may not be an accountant, Sloan,' said the superintendent dangerously, 'but I am not a fool. Surely that sort of money would show up in the figures?'

Detective Inspector Sloan sighed. 'I'm afraid, sir, that the figures for the Lake Ryrie Reserve were wrong. And it was when they showed up wrong that the trouble began.'

'And that's what the girl spotted?'

Sloan nodded sadly. 'I expect she thought it was just a simple clerical error so she made the mistake of telephoning Howard Air to check.'

'And wrote her own death warrant by doing so?'

'I'm afraid so. The telephonist at Pearson, Worrow and Gisby had noted the call, though.'

'And all Air had to do in response to Jill Carter's query was agree with her that there had been a mistake?'

'I'm sure that's what he did in the first place. Probably laughed it off and blamed the typist.'

'And whom should he have blamed?' Leeyes never ever for one moment took his eye off the ball.

'The accident to the senior audit clerk at the accountants, David Barton. That was what started it all. He was the one there who Howard Air was in cahoots with. Not the partners.'

'The man who's still unconscious?'

'Him. It was that and the fact that Wayne Goddard went to look at Whimbrel House on Tuesday with Sid Wetherspoon that really sent the balloon up.'

'Ah.'

'We don't know for certain but I imagine that Goddard, who was a drug pusher in a very small way, recognized all the signs . . .'

'And smells. Don't forget that some drugs smell, Sloan.'

'And then made the mistake of telling someone higher up the drug chain that he now knew where their distribution was done from.'

'Not very clever.'

'He wasn't. But someone was. Very.'

'So both the people who knew anything were killed then?'

'Yes, sir. We think the girl was abducted in the pub car park as she left – Nigel Worrow stayed on a bit and didn't see the going of her – and that she was killed at Whimbrel House.'

'She would have accepted the offer of a lift home from the Ornum Arms car park from Howard Air,' agreed Leeyes sagely. 'Only natural.'

'So her body was at Whimbrel House, which they were going to have to stop using pretty soon anyway.' Sloan attempted to continue his narration.

'Because Wayne Goddard knew about it?'

'That's one reason,' said Sloan.

'Everyone would know Goddard wasn't reliable,' pointed out Leeyes. 'Stood out a mile. I can see that he would have to go.'

'There was another reason,' said Sloan, explaining that sooner or later Peter Caversham would have to be accepted as the legal owner of Whimbrel House. 'And he would be even less reliable,' said Sloan. 'He's a total wreck, but that wouldn't have stopped him inheriting the settled estate.'

'From what you say about him, Sloan, the drug people would have known that themselves.'

'Yes, sir. Getting Jill Carter's body out of the house in the mummy case was a good way of starting a fresh hare as well.'

'When in doubt,' declared Superintendent Leeyes, a long-term veteran of the Berebury Town Council's Watch Committee, 'confuse the issue.'

'Stirring up the coroner did that, too,' said Sloan. 'Queered the pitch nicely by making us suspect Marcus Fixby-Smith, among other things, but the real reason was so that Howard Air would know how the investigation was going. Don't forget he was Chairman of the Museum Committee.'

'I wonder if Locombe-Stableford's taking drugs,' said Leeyes thoughtfully. 'You never know these days, do you?'

Sloan hurried into speech. 'This man Barton, sir, from the accountants . . .'

'Ah, yes. Where does he come in?'

'He prepared the Lake Ryrie figures for Jim Pearson to sign.'

'I thought you said they didn't amount to much.'

'They didn't on the accounts Jim Pearson signed off.'

'But?'

'But the accounts that went to the Calleshire County Bank to authorize sending the money out to Lasserta had three zeros restored to the top of the column.'

'Three zeros.' The superintendent raised a podgy hand. 'Don't tell me, Sloan. Let me guess. Standing for thousands, I take it?'

'That's right, sir. Jim Pearson didn't expect to find them on his copy and they weren't there. The bank did and the thousands sign was at the top of the columns on the copy that went there. The bank, you see, had reason to know that Howard Air was both rich and generous.'

'That should have alerted them,' said Leeyes unfairly. 'It's not a combination you often see.'

'No, sir.'

'Simple, when you come to think of it.'

'Well, it's one way to launder more than three-quarters of a million pounds each year,' said Sloan sedately.

'No wonder he could afford to try to bribe you, Sloan.'

'Peanuts to him, sir.' He took a breath. 'But I should have spotted that Air was up to mischief myself earlier: there was no call for him to have been at the accountants' yesterday when we got there.'

'That's not evidence.'

'And, sir, I should have picked up that he was coughing a lot then.' The hospital had told him that earlier diagnosis probably wouldn't make any difference to the dolorous outcome of Howard Air's chest illness. 'I didn't think . . .'

'Coughing? What on earth are you talking about, Sloan?'

'Howard Air was ill in bed when we got to his house, sir.'

'Nothing trivial, I hope?'

'Very serious indeed, sir, the hospital say. He's caught anthrax from handling the mummy. The pulmonary variety. It's like pneumonia, only worse. Dr Dabbe says the disease is always on the cards if you don't take the proper precautions when handling the contents of a mummy case.'

'The curse of the Pharaohs, Sloan.' The superintendent didn't sound unduly regretful.

Detective Inspector Sloan, still smarting at the insult of attempted bribery, said, 'I rather like to think of it as the long arm of justice myself, sir.'

'Another way, Crosby, in which Howard Air was able to convert cash into an asset,' said Sloan, 'was by buying the Kirk sisters' nephew's endowment insurance policy from him.'

'I don't get it, sir.' The detective constable's brow clouded over.

'It's known as a viatical settlement,' said Sloan, fresh from a tutorial from a mightily relieved Jim Pearson. 'And it's quite legal.'

'Come again, sir.'

'When Derek died, all that Howard Air had to do as the last owner of the policy was to send Derek's death certificate to the insurance company and sit back and wait for a large cheque to come through.'

'Nice work, if you can get it,' said Crosby.

'Of clean money,' underlined Sloan. The superintendent had cottoned on to this more quickly than Crosby had but Sloan was still feeling benevolent towards the detective constable.

'Smelling of roses, I shouldn't be surprised,' said

Crosby. 'Like his aunts. They didn't have a clue that the heroin was parked at their sanctuary when it came ashore.'

'The dogs that did bark in the night,' said Sloan. 'Mind you, Pearson and Worrow guessed that was what Derek had done, although they didn't know who had bought the policy.'

'Catch them shopping a client . . .'

'All the same, the accountants should have told the proper authorities they suspected something,' said Sloan righteously. 'So we'd better let Colin Thornhill go now, hadn't we, sir? Before he sues us for wrongful arrest . . .'

'This is Berebury District General Hospital. Is Detective Inspector Sloan available to take a call?' said a woman's voice.

'Speaking,' said Sloan, suppressing a yawn brought about by an unhealthy combination of tiredness and hunger.

'That you, Sloan?' said another voice. 'Dabbe here. Just reporting on that post-mortem.'

'Which one?' enquired Detective Inspector Sloan. There had, after all, been rather a lot of them this week in which the police had had more than a passing interest.

'Rodoheptah. We had to put him on the back burner when the Goddard body came in.'

Sloan could have wished for a happier metaphor, but he held his peace.

'We've just got him down as Rodoheptah. Is that right? We don't have a Christian name.'

'He wasn't Christian.' Offhand, Sloan couldn't think of whom or what Rodoheptah would have worshipped: Ra, the sun god, most probably. Or had it been Osiris, ruler of the hereafter?

'Sorry, I was forgetting. Anyway,' the doctor airily dismissed theism and went back to his own subject, 'the post-mortem examination was very interesting. These palaeopathologists certainly know their stuff.'

Sloan said he was glad to hear it.

'Of course, with a truly mummified body there is quite a lot of material preserved that is lost in the ordinary way.'

Sloan wasn't at all sure that he wanted to think about the ordinary way. Certainly not as applied to Jill Carter, innocent victim, and Wayne Goddard, not so innocent victim but still not deserving of an early death. Or Peter Caversham, as good as half dead.

'All of which means,' continued the pathologist, 'that Professor Miles Upton and I have been able to identify the probable cause of his death.'

'Really, doctor?' Sloan pulled his notebook towards him and tried to take a proper interest in the year 2000 BC or thereabouts.

'Sand.'

'Sand?'

'And the dry dusty climate. Sandstorms would have been a great trouble to him. Difficult to get away from it, there.'

'I can see that, doctor, but . . .'

'Leading in the case of this mummy to sand pneumo-coniosis. Professor Upton found massive fibrosis of the lungs, which I was able to confirm endoscopically. And we've just had the histology report back.'

It was a disease of the lung that was going to kill Howard Air, too, thought Detective Inspector Sloan as he made another note. Pollution of one sort or another was an older problem than he had imagined, then. Murder, on the other hand, wasn't. The ancient Egyptians had always experienced murder – and worse, much worse.

'Sand was ever their great difficulty out there,' the pathologist was saying. 'They couldn't prevent it getting into their food as well as their lungs and the grit ground their teeth down.'

'Which must have made eating difficult,' said Sloan, conscious that he himself was in real need of food now.

'Very.'

'So the coroner can have his post-mortem report after all,' mused Sloan. And, although he didn't say so, the superintendent his Sunday morning's round of golf.

'On an adult male, aged about thirty, date of death unknown,' said the pathologist.

'Isn't science wonderful?' murmured Sloan, deciding that perhaps they would have their kitchen floor covering renewed. It was, after all, important to keep matters in proportion . . .